AUG 2 2 2018
P9-BYV-838

PEN AMERICA BEST DEBUT SHORT STORIES 2018

PEN AMERICA BEST DEBUT SHORT STORIES 2018

EDITED BY
YUKA IGARASHI

JUDGES
JODI ANGEL
LESLEY NNEKA ARIMAH
ALEXANDRA KLEEMAN

First published in the United States in 2018 by Catapult (catapult.co)

Please see Permissions on page 205 for individual credits.

ISBN: 978-1-936787-93-7

Catapult titles are distributed to the trade by Publishers Group West
Phone: 866-400-5351

Library of Congress Control Number: 2018938839

Printed in the United States of America
10 9 8 7 6 5 4 3 2 1

CONTENTS

INTRODUCTION

THE STORIES IN this anthology are by writers whose fiction appeared in print or online for the first time in 2017. They were selected for publication, out of thousands of submissions, by magazine editors who likely had never read the writers before. They were then chosen for the PEN/Robert J. Dau Short Story Prize for Emerging Writers, from 150 nominations, by three judges who have recently written their own award-winning story collections. They represent the newest fiction being published today that has made the most lasting impression on a chain of careful readers. Ezra Pound wrote that literature is "news that stays news"; these stories bring us the latest news.

Each piece included here is surprising and unique in approach and effect. Still, when read collectively, certain themes emerge. I noticed that there are a lot of performers in these pages. Some are in costume: Jeremy, dressed as a Hercules mascot at Magic Kingdom in Ernie Wang's "Stay Brave, My Hercules"; the couple in Maud Streep's "The Crazies," who play a corset-wearing whore and a chaps-wearing cowboy in a ghost town in Montana. There are singers and dancers, vulnerable and triumphant and memorable: in Lauren Friedlander's "Bellevonia Beautee," two young "beautees" practice kicks and shimmies and vocals for what is supposedly a singing group led by a man named Andy; in Cristina Fríes's "New Years in La Calera," a young "campesina" in a remote valley in the Andes dances to cumbia while guerrilla soldiers point guns at her.

Even characters who aren't playacting or putting on a show

are concerned with scripts, with hitting the right notes. "Zombie Horror" by Drew McCutchen is narrated by a caseworker for the recently undead. He doesn't have much experience with zombie counseling, so he relies on pamphlets and weekly training emails from his department to tell him what to say to his dirt-covered, half-decayed clients to help them readjust to being alive. ("You *must* talk to them quietly. They've been used to quiet for so long.") He does intake in front of a one-way mirror so his colleagues can watch his technique—his audience.

Three pieces frame migration as a performance. Ava Tomasula y Garcia's "Videoteca Fin del Mundo" is about migrants detained at the U.S.-Mexico border while escaping violence in their home countries. In many cases, they are incarcerated in "hieleras" (freezers) and "perreras" (doghouses) and offered no legal help as they face their asylum hearings. The piece came out of the author's real-life work with the Asylum Seeker Advocacy Project, where she saw firsthand how individuals are made to "audition for the part of Refugee." "Can you play the character they are looking for at your Credible Fear interview?" Tomasula y Garcia writes. "This is the only time your humanness will be based on your dehumanization, so barter for it and say only what they want to hear."

In "Six Months" by Celeste Mohammed, another "illegal" finds himself auditioning to stay in the country. After losing his engineering job and running out of options for supporting his common-law wife and two sons, Junior flies from Trinidad to New York to live with a cousin and work at a supermarket. When he notices that Becky the cashier has a crush on him, he embarks on an ethically compromised, strategically dubious plan to seduce and marry her before his temporary visa runs out—all while keeping her a secret from (and continuing to provide for) his family back home. If the refugees in "Videoteca Fin del Mundo" are required to display the correct kind of desperation, Junior's act is about concealing desperation—being the blank slate we often want our immigrants to be. "You just have this gut feeling things will go better for you, in America, if you hang a fuckin' sign round your neck: COME IN. I OPEN . . . TO EVERYTHING." The immigrants in Megan Tucker's "Candidates" also invent more acceptable, less precarious versions of themselves for the world, though they do it by adding to rather than subtracting from their family. The story is told from the point of view of two sisters who are waiting at home for a man to come over and buy a used crib. Their mother has turned the TV on in the empty den and closed the door, to make the buyer believe there's a father in the room.

We typically think of a performance as something that happens within a limited time frame—an intake interview, a furniture sale. It's a heightened state, set apart from "ordinary" life. But what's most interesting in these stories is the way a performance seeps into life. The frame blurs and the stage dissolves. Back at Magic Kingdom, when Jeremy-as-Hercules makes friends with a wheelchair-bound Make-A-Wish kid, he's thinking about his partner, dying of cancer at home; when he smiles and flexes and repeats Disney-approved messages to "be strong" and "be brave," he's also talking to himself. Once summer ends, the ghost-town cowboy and whore from "The Crazies" settle down in a house in the mountains and continue their reenactment for each other: "I had wanted to be the kind of wife who'd bring down an elk one day and cook it the next, in lingerie and a flannel shirt," the narrator says.

Another character in a wife costume appears in Lin King's "Appetite." Shortly after her twenty-fourth birthday, Mayling's mother demands that she find a husband from among the "optometrists, patent lawyers, accountants, chemical engineering PhDs" that make up her family's social circle in Taiwan. She finally chooses Shutian, a dentist. On their wedding night, she's in a crisp white nightgown like "a heroine from a Gothic novel"; she tries kissing her husband "as she had seen kissers do in countless Hollywood films." The soft rock piping through the couple's home obscures the lack of conversation; soon enough, children arrive, and decades pass as Mayling dutifully plays the roles expected of her in her marriage and her family.

Mayling's lifelong costume does eventually show its seams, just as the "Dale Evans drag" starts to slip for the narrator in "The Crazies." If the stories here reveal how we become the selves we perform, they also reveal the instability of that becoming. The self is an ever-changing construction, continually attempting and faltering at coherence. There is a visual manifestation of this in Alex Terrell's "Black Dog": the protagonist, Io, is followed around wherever she goes by other phantom Ios—Io-Leather-Skirt, Io-in-Jeans, Io-in-Red at a rooftop party; Ios dressed in white as she wanders into the woods. Elinam Agbo's "1983" describes a different kind of fractured self. The story begins with the narrator walking through fog, squinting at a hazy figure down the road. She's in a village in Ghana during a famine, and she vaguely remembers a husband, work in the city, a missing aunt—but the holes in her mind prevent her from knowing any more about who she is.

But there is freedom and possibility in not knowing. "Brent, Bandit King" by Grayson Morley is narrated by something called a Facilitator—the artificial intelligence of a computer program that adaptively responds to the actions chosen by players of a role-playing video game. The Facilitator is aware of all the branching story paths and outcomes available to the players inside the game, but it is limited by what [Brent], its player, wants to do—and [Brent] only wants to pick up weapons and kill other bandits. Of all the characters and performers within this book, the Facilitator is the only one that can't, and doesn't, ever deviate from script. All it can do is keep reminding [Brent] that [Brent] can: "I was hoping that, together, we might break free of the likely actions. We might traverse a less probable narrative path, find ourselves an [Uncommon Ending]." In one way or another, every story in this collection is reminding us of this too. I'm grateful to the Dau family, to PEN America, to our judges, to the original editors of these twelve exceptional works, and, finally, to the writers themselves, for helping to deliver this good news.

YUKA IGARASHI
Series Editor

PEN AMERICA BEST DEBUT SHORT STORIES 2018

EDITOR'S NOTE

Experience tells us it's probably not going to work out. Yet every time we open a new submission, we bring fresh hope to the page along with some measure of hesitation. Every one of us who read "Six Months"—beginning with our fiction editor and a couple of crackerjack interns—found our way past that hesitation after the first few lines, and by the end we were in knots. Luther's visa was just about to expire and his two worlds were on the verge of a collision that would ruin them both. Here was a story we were all excited to publish in *NER*. But did we trust ourselves; had we really just struck unsolicited-submission gold? Who was this writer? Was this dialect accurate, or even authentic? In the end, none of that even mattered, because by the time we finished reading we were entirely convinced by the story itself. It was as if we'd just spent time in Luther Archibald Junior's presence as he told us about his harrowing misadventures in New York. We believed him, and we believed in this writer.

As it happens, Celeste Mohammed, who was born and raised in Trinidad, had to overcome some internalized censorship of her own to get this voice onto the page, and we think she succeeded beautifully.

It also seems worth noting that we accepted this story—a highly empathic story about "illegals"—on inauguration day in 2017.

Carolyn Kuebler, editor
New England Review

SIX MONTHS

Celeste Mohammed

WHEN OIL DROP to 9US$ a barrel, man, you know you getting lay off. The only question is when. Like everybody else in the industry, you wait.

It come like the worst thing that could happen, when they announce people going "in tranches" every month.

At first, every time you don't get a envelope, you breathe a sigh of relief. After a while, though, you start feeling like a death row inmate in a cell near the gallows; like these bitches want you to witness everybody else execution. Soon, the fact you still working come like a noose swinging in front your face, grazing your nose. You start to wish they just get it over with.

And when it happen, you rush home to Judith, your common-law wife, mother of your two children, and give her the news. She put her hand on her heart and say, "We could breathe easy now, Junior. We could move on."

You and Judith cling to each other there in the kitchen. You feel your prick resurrecting like Lazarus. Is months since the last time. You know Judith feeling it too. She pulling away? No, she gripping on tighter.

You's a trembling schoolboy again, mouth watering over hers

as you grab deep inside that housedress like is a bran tub. You find her panty-crotch and rake it aside. Right there on the counter, next to the toaster, it happen. Two jook and a tremble and everything done. But Judith don't seem to mind. She patting your back, stroking your hair, till your breathing slow down. Then she whisper she going for the boys.

You swagger to the bedroom. Dive on the bed, hug the pillow, and smile. You not too worried. The severance pay was a good chunk—it'll hold you for a while. Besides, you tell yourself, it don't matter how low oil go; Trinidad need man like me. They can't shut down every rig, every factory. Nah! METs will always find work.

But then April turn to May, May turn to June, and still nobody hiring mechanical engineering technicians. The talk everywhere is recession, recession. Judith still have her receptionist job in the doctor-office and y'all could probably manage a li'l while longer. But what really starting to hurt is your pride. You's a big, hardstones man and watch you: every day, waking up with the house empty and a note from Judith on the table. Cook, clean, wash, iron—you do everything she say.

Until one night, when Judith squat over your face and say "suck it," you shove her off and say, "Suck it your damn self. I's not your bitch."

YOU CALL YOUR cousin Rufus, in New York. America have the most factories. Rufus name "citizen," he must know somebody to offer you something under the table.

Three days later, he call back. Good news. If you organize

your visa and ticket and get there by September month-end, they'll squeeze you in at the S-Town Supermarket near his house, in Queens. "Engineering work?" you say. And the man say no, is the meat room. You tell Rufus, "Yeah," but, same speed, you hang up and tell Judith, "He mad or what? I have education!"

You plan to wait couple weeks, then say you didn't get the visa. Meantime, you drop your tail between your leg and call your eighteen-year-old baby sister, Gail.

"You think you could ask that old man something for me?"

"A job, nah?" Gail say, like she was waiting on the call.

"Yeah, girl. Things hard. You know I's not the kind to ask Mr. H for favors. But them Syrians, they own everything. See what you could do, nah?"

Imagine *you* asking Gail for help. After you never do one ass for her. After you did move out and leave her with that drunk skunk, your father, Luther Sr.

When she first hook up with Mr. H, that married asshole, it did make you feel to vomit: your li'l sister spreading her legs for him, for his money. You did tell Judith as much and she say, "Well, talk to Gail. You's she big brother."

But you did say, "Nah, is not my place." And is true. Gail was fuckin' for betterment. How you coulda ever face her and say, *Don't*, when Mr. H was the one minding her: putting a roof over her head, food on her table, clothes on her back, making she feel classy, giving she a start in life. That's more than you—Mr. Big Brother—or your waste-a-time father ever do for the li'l girl. *Shame!*

Next day, Gail call back: "Sorry, boy. Hard luck."

You wonder if she even ask.

One night, after everybody fall asleep, you packing away the school books your son Jason leave on the dining table. Flipping through his sketch pad, a heading in red catch your eye: *My Family.* Four stick figures in scratchy crayon clothes. You's the tallest and next to your watermelon head it have a arrow and a label: *Luther Jr. Stay-at-home Dad.* In your hand it have something that resemble . . . a axe? a boat paddle? Nah, you realize is a spatula.

"Fuck," you mumble, pulling out a chair and sinking in it. Your son gone and ask the teacher what to call you, now that you's scratch your balls for a living.

"JUNIOR, YOU SURE you want to do this?" Judith say. She straining macaroni in the sink; you grating cheese. "America ain't no bed-a-rose, nah!" she add.

You argue back and forth 'bout all the people she know that gone America and dying to come back.

Then—*thunk!*—Judith rest-down the strainer hard in the sink. You glance across. She staring out the window.

"You go miss me? That's what it is, ain't? Tell me."

"Don't be a ass!" she say. "I's a big woman, I could handle myself. But, is the boys . . ."

"Let we cross that bridge when we get to it," you say, a tightness in your chest like you just bench-press 150. "I don't even have a visa yet."

You go down a li'l stronger on the grater. This fuckin' woman hard! Harder than this old, dry cheese. It woulda kill her to say she go miss you?

The two of you was seventeen, in the last year of technical school, when she get pregnant with Jason. Y'all wasn't in love or nothing, but her parents put her out, so you had to band together. *Your* parents was a disgrace: Luther Sr. drowning in puncheon-rum, and your mother, Janice, ups-and-gone with a next man. Three years pass you straight, like a full bus. Then Judith find out she pregnant again, with Kevin. You and Judith, it come like y'all grow up together. And, although you's a big man now, twenty-four years, you never had to face the outside world without Judith. She raise your babies and, in a way, she raise you too.

She never been the lovey-dovey kind but, man, she get more colder lately. She dropping words for you; saying things like, "People can't make love on hungry belly."

YOU PAY FOR the appointment, fill out the form, take the picture. You photocopy a bank statement, fake a job letter. You line up in the road at 5 a.m., in front the US Embassy, with a sandwich and a juice box in your jacket.

People in the line *shoo-shoo*-ing. Uncle Sam know everything is what they saying. Hmmm. Suppose the embassy ask 'bout your aunt who did overstay her six months in LA? Suppose they know you lose your real job?

When your batch of twenty get call-in the embassy, you watch everything. People go up once to hand in their documents. Then again for the interview. You figure out those getting send by the post office counter is the lucky ones. Them others, who drop their eyes and slink out quick, quick, them is the rejects.

You watch five from your batch get reject—some of them real posh looking.

Shit! If they could do them that, who's me? You feeling like you have to pee but you dare not leave your seat.

At 9:00, they call your name; 9:15, the interview start.

The lady barely watching you. She asking simple questions but you feel like she just waiting for you to trip up. When she ask, "Purpose of visit?" you amaze yourself with how you slant the lie you and Judith did practice ("vacation"). How you pull it nearer the truth.

"School purchases," you say in your best English, "before September. The children needs plenty things."

The lady smile. "They always do," she say.

Your B1/B2 visa get approve.

You feel high and light—like you could reach America on your own fuckin' wings. You stop at KFC, near City Gate, and splurge: a bucket, four regular sides, a two-liter Sprite. A nice surprise for the boys after school. On the maxi-taxi ride home, you decide how you going to tell them.

JASON RIPPING INTO his second piece. Kevin still nibbling a drumstick. You watch all their hand and face getting greasy and sticky; the ketchup plopping down on their vests. Scabby knee, shred-up elbow, Jason missing teeth, Kevin always-runny nose. Is like you recording a movie in your head, to replay later, in America. They sit, stand, climb, all over the dining-table chairs, while Judith complaining and wiping, wiping.

Finally, you say, "Boys, what if we could eat KFC every Friday?"

Not even glancing up from his meat, Jason answer, "I done ask Mummy that long time and she say we can't afford it."

"I know. But we could afford it now. Daddy going America."

The boys stare at you blank, blank.

"Allyuh have to make a list of all the toys allyuh want. Because, when I go America, I getting *everything*." You growl the last word, bare your teeth, like a hungry lion.

The cubs laugh.

"America far?" Jason say.

"Yes, I have to go on a big airplane."

"We could go too?"

"No, you have school. Plus you have to take care of your mother." You glance at Judith. She look like she holding her breath. In truth, you doing the same damn thing.

"So, Daddy," Jason say, "when you say 'everything' you mean I could get a G.I. Joe watch?"

The boys call toy after toy, snack after snack—everything they know from American TV. With every yes, their excitement grow and grow. Till they fidgeting again—more than ever now—popping up like bubbles in the Sprite. They start rocking the chairs and singing, "Daddy going America! Daddy going America!" They making you feel like you's a superhero.

"Stop it!" Judith shout. "Stop that right now!"

A FEW WEEKS later, in the purple-looking hours before dawn, you slink out your bed and into the boys' bedroom. You tiptoe and kiss Jason, on the top bunk; you bend and kiss Kevin, his cheek wet with dribble. You want them wake up so you could hear them say, "Bye, Daddy," but, same time, you scared they will. You *might* be able to bear it. Or you might just say, "Fuck America," and stay.

In the stillness, you hear a engine purr and handbrakes jerk. Your brother-in-law, Declan, just pull up outside.

Judith with you by the kitchen table, going over everything one last time: ticket, departure card, Rufus address, virgin passport. You tuck them inside the same bomber jacket you did wear to the embassy.

Your almost-empty suitcase standing up by the door—halfway in, halfway out—like it have two minds 'bout this whole thing. You and Judith hug and you kiss her on the cheek. Then, you put her at arm's length. Is time to go—Declan waiting—but the last seven years, they come like glue. Your palms not budging from the sleeve of Judith nightie.

You fake a grin and say, "Take care of them li'l fellas, eh."

And you linger, hoping she say something tender; so you could say something tender too. Something like *I frighten* or *I will miss you.*

But it don't happen. So you just leave Judith right there, leaning on the doorframe like she propping up the house.

OCTOBER 1, YOU touch down in JFK. The place big, big, big and bright, bright, bright. It come like you in one of them sci-fi movies where they land the plane inside a spaceship. Only shiny metal and white light.

Everybody else seem to know where they going so you fall in and follow the crowd. In the immigration line, your heart racing just like in the embassy—like you guilty of something. The officer asking almost the same questions and you give the same answers. He do so—*bam!*—and stamp your passport for six months. *Hallelujah!*

You find your suitcase in no time—thanks to the orange ribbon

Judith did tie on it. Then, the crowd take you past the customs desk and through a wall of doors that just open up by itself.

You in a big, wide clearing with metal barriers all 'round. Just beyond, it have at least three rows of faces and signs, plenty hand-made signs. And plenty eyes aiming at you, but looking past you—you's not who they want. You freeze on the spot, like fuckin' stage fright. You trying to sift through, to find that one face, the only one you know in New York City. Seconds ticking and your spit drying out on your tongue like rain on the road. What if he forget?

"Junior! Yo, Junior! Over here!" Rufus find you. He a li'l way off to the side of the crowd waving, like he signaling a plane.

"Welcome to the US of A!" he say, hugging you hard.

"Thanks, man. Thanks," you say.

Is a long, hot drive to Queens. Why the ass Rufus don't put on the air condition? But he saying is the last summer weather so enjoy it while you can.

The air different, kinda crispy. But you surprised how dull and dingy the place looking. Brown everywhere. And kinda factory-ish—big, big chimney and pipe and lorry in every yard. A small hope start bleeping inside you—maybe you'll find MET work here; maybe this grocery thing is just a start.

Then, the streets get narrow and you reading signs: check-cashing, car wash, Rite Aid, eyebrow threading. What the ass is eyebrow threading? And where all the damn white people? You thought New York streets would be crawling with them, but you only seeing brown faces, like yours.

Another right turn and is strictly houses now—all the same type but different colors. Rufus stop and get out to open a saggy chain link gate.

Rotting garbage sneaking up in your nose-hole. It have to be garbage. It can't be shit, right? This is America, for chrissake. Still, you don't say nothing to Rufus because you don't want to embarrass the man. You get your suitcase and follow him.

"But this is one big, *macco* house you have here, Rufus!"

"Yeah," he say, "Top-floor rented out to some Jamaicans. But I hooked you up, cuz. You got the whole basement to yourself."

The basement turn out to be some pipes and pillars, a rust-bitten washing machine and dryer, a plain cement floor. But in one corner, near the stairs, it have a crooked, wooden room leaning up on the concrete wall. As Rufus unlocking the door he grin just like your son Kevin and say, "Built this myself. Used to rent it to a Paki, but I threw him out for you."

It don't have much in the room. A patchy old couch (Rufus show you how to fold it out to a bed), a TV, another contraption he say is a electric heater, a closet and a musty smell. But say what: you in America! That's the only damn thing that matter.

Rufus say, "Look, I gotta bounce, kid. Shift starts at six. Take a nap or whatever. If you're hungry, help yourself to anything upstairs."

"I could call home?" you say.

Rufus open his wallet and flip a card in your direction. Turning away, he say, "Just read the back and follow the instructions. Phone's in the kitchen. You're gonna have to stock up on that shit."

"First thing tomorrow," you say, running up the stairs behind him.

"And remember, the deal is . . ."

"Yeah, I know: basement free this first month; buy my own food; two hundred a month after that."

"A'ight," Rufus say. He point to the phone on the wall and duck out the side door.

Leg-shaking, you dial; following the voice instructions, waiting for the international beep, praying you didn't mess up.

"Hello," Judith answer.

Boom! You could jump for joy.

"I reach," you say.

"Hello? Junior?"

"Yeah, is me. I reach."

"Junior? Hello?"

You shouting in the receiver but Judith still not hearing you.

WORK AT THE grocery start bright and early the next day. It turn out not to be in the meat room. Ahmed, the manager, save that better-paying job for a fella from his own country, Palestine. You get the $4.25-a-hour job packing shelves and swiping goods with a li'l sticker-gun.

Becky is a cashier. The only white girl. She think she down with all the other cashiers but you hear them laughing behind her back and calling her "fat white trash."

That evening, you decide to buy some groceries. It late, the store ready to close. Becky is the only one still open. As you set down your things she say, "You don't talk much, do you, Island Man?"

You laugh.

"Ah! See, he smiles!" she say, and you smile a li'l wider. "So, you got a family back home?" she ask.

"Two boys."

"Lucky bastard. How old?"

"Seven and four."

"Miss 'em yet?"

You nod.

"Married?"

"Nah." Technically, is the truth. But a truth with plenty holes in it, like the netting on this paw-paw you buying. You smile in a guilty way. But Becky blushing, as if your smile have something to do with her. *Ha, Lord! This fat-girl think you desperate or what?*

She making small talk, punching in prices—mostly from memory. But then you notice she skipping over some things, just pushing them down the belt. You think is a mistake—she must be distracted with all the chitchat—so you stretch out your hand to stop the next can. Becky watch you dead in the eye and wink.

You bag your groceries and burn road home.

You boil water and make some Top Ramen. Chili-lime shrimp. The thing smelling like fuckin' insecticide—tasting worse—but at least it warm. You eat on the edge of the sofa bed, watching the TV, but really the damn thing watching you 'cause your mind so fuckin' far right now.

This is the first time you ever thief anything in life. Suppose Ahmed find out and call the police? Suppose they post your ass back to Trinidad? Imagine you: in a vest, short pants, and handcuffs, waddling off the plane; your boys ducking down 'cause they shame. You decide never to do this thing again—never, ever. And you decide to pay it back by working extra hard and doing anything the boss ask you to do. You will make yourself Ahmed li'l bitch.

And—*shit!*—you keep that promise. You punch your card every day at seven and punch out every night at nine. Sometimes you doing double shifts. Sometimes you covering for people. Still, every red cent of your weekly salary spend-out before you even get it. It have Rufus rent to pay, Judith money to send, and you trying to full a barrel with food-and-thing to ship home for Christmas. A few groceries for yourself now and then—soup, bread, cheese—but, for a fella in your situation, phone cards is Life. America over-lonely. Just work, work, work, then this empty room. So you don't mind: you would rather starve than not hear your children.

BECKY, SHE REALIZE you don't take no lunch break. She ask 'bout it one day and you brush her off with a weak joke: you maintaining your physique. Couple days later—lunchtime self—you taking a smoke outside with Carlos, the Dominican fella from Produce.

"Ma-a-n," he say, "you peep that sexy new *morena* 'cross the street at the dry cleaners?"

"Nah, which one that is, boy?"

"Short. Thick. *Tremendo culo.*" He move his hands like he tracing a big, round pumpkin.

"Oh, she? Yeah, I glimpse her yesterday. But that's not my scene, brother."

"Whattaya mean, *amigo*? You don't see that ass?"

You laugh and explain, "I not really into fat girls, you know, Carlos. Gimme the smallies, the chicken-wings. You see how I *magga*? I like girls to suit my size. When a woman drop she leg on me in the night, I mustn't dead in my sleep."

Carlos slapping his thigh and dancing around. He swear you's the funniest man he ever meet. Chilling out like this, talking big—the way you does talk back home—and having somebody appreciate you for it. It real nice. A nice change from licking American ass whole day: *Yes, the brussels sprouts is right this way, ma'am . . . No, sir, don't worry, I'll clean that mess right up.*

A noise come from behind, inside the loading bay. You spin 'round; Becky standing up there clutching a li'l Ziploc bag with both hands.

Oh, fuck! Maybe she hear what you just say 'bout fat girls? Apart from Carlos, she's your only friend here. You don't want to hurt her feelings.

Becky just giggle, "Oops! Male-bonding," hand you the sandwich, and walk off, back to her register. Each half of her bottom trembling to a different beat, like they suffering from two separate earthquakes.

You like Becky. She real easygoing. Always happy, always joking. When she laugh, she does make a noise like hiccups and her freckles does bounce like they in a Carnival band. But, you starting to get the vibes that Becky want you to *love* her.

She say she from Pennsylvania. Thirty-five, never married, no kids. She living with roommates, a bunch of other "ex-Amish girls" catching up on life. You don't know much 'bout Amish people except what you see on TV: they does pray plenty, farm plenty, and they don't like outsiders. *You* must be as outsider as it get, so you very surprised that Becky always squeezing in a line or two 'bout how *black men are so hot* and how *the Caribbean accent is so sexy.* Like is only one fuckin' accent for everybody in the whole Caribbean Sea. *Steups!*

One day, Becky come out plain, plain and ask, "So, you're not married, but is there . . . anyone? Special, I mean?"

You hear yourself say, "Special? Nah. Just my children-mother." And you almost expect a cock to crow because you feel like Judas

Fuckin' Iscariot. You don't know why you keep doing this shit! Hiding Judith. But you just have this gut feeling things will go better for you, in America, if you hang a sign round your neck: COME IN. I OPEN . . . TO EVERYTHING.

RUFUS HOME ON his off night and y'all watching *Die Hard with a Vengeance* on his illegal pay-per-view. You tell him 'bout Becky. "My man!" he say. "That's your meal-ticket, yo!"

When you look confuse, he spell it out in neon. "Nigga, you better fuck that white heifer and get yourself straight. Yeah, they gave you six months. But you can flip that into a lifetime, with a green card."

Frowning, you wonder if you hear right. Rufus know Judith; he does stay by your house every Carnival; he's eat her food; and she does much-him-up. They kinda close. You start to wonder if Judith set him up to test you or something.

"The fuck you looking at me like that for?" Rufus say. "I ain't telling you fall in love with the bitch. I'm saying: make *her* love you. Opportunity's knocking and you need to respond, nigga. Think about your family."

You still gaping at Rufus like you no hablas ingles. He shrug and done the talk, "People get married for papers all the time, cuz. This the US of A, remember."

Your mind sign off from Bruce Willis problems. You glimpsing now that you been thinking way too small 'bout yours. Why keep sending your family sandwich money when you could bring them to a fuckin' banquet?

Rufus damn right: being here in America ain't about your

preference. What kinda girls you like or what kinda work you qualified for. Is about keeping yourself ready: knees bent, palms cupped. And juicing the fuck out of every opportunity that drop down.

Make Becky love you, Rufus did say. Make she love you till she would do anything to keep you. Sign on that dotted line, even. Yeah, you could do that. But you have to work quick—only five months left.

Later that night, you start feeling shaky 'bout your decision, so you call home.

Judith hear the beep and bawl, "Boys! Come quick! Is allyuh father." The connection real good this time: you actually hear their rubber slippers going *plap, plap, plap*. Some rustling; a couple thuds—they fighting for the phone. Jason win and Kevin start to cry. While Judith petting him, you ask Jason 'bout school, if he behaving himself.

"A boy did push li'l Kevin down in school," he say. "But I find the fella and push him back harder." He singing the whole story in his high-pitch voice.

"Good," you say, "stick up for him, eh. Always. You name Big Brother."

Then you talk to Kevin. He parrot everything his big brother just say, only with a lisp. As you listen, you close your eyes. Rufus right: is not about just feeding them. If you bring them to America you could give them what Luther Sr. and Janice never give you and Gail: a head start in life.

Then, Judith come on. She do a quick run-through: your mother and sister doing good, light bill and cable bill paid up, no water because the landlord didn't pay the bill, send the money Western Union next time (MoneyGram line always too long).

She on top of everything. Super-capable. That's how it is with Judith. She don't neglect a single duty, but she does make you feel bad for making her do it—like you's not enough man. Before you fly-out, she did open her legs for you, but she never make a fuckin' sound. She hard.

Her voice change now, though—low and trembling—when she say, "It had another shooting. Right outside the school. The snow cone vendor. They say he was a gang member."

"The boys see?" you ask, hoarse, because you frighten and you choking on it like stale bread.

"Nah. They was in class, thank God. But still, Junior . . ."

"I know, I know."

Jason and Kevin. You could send them all the money in America; that can't block them from a Pleasantview bullet.

WINTER COMING FAST. Your first. Your nose bleeding every time you step outside, your skin gray and itchy. You never been this fuckin' cold. And you miss your sons so bad it come like a toothache that does fill up your head and get worse and worse every day.

Soon, the bomber jacket not cutting it no more. Rufus lend you some stuff—coat, gloves, scarf, beanie—and you find some boots in the thrift store on Merrick Boulevard. Hand-me-downs, but fuck that! You stepping high these days, since Laparkan Shipping collect the barrel you was filling. Six weeks, they say—it'll get to Trinidad in time for Christmas.

Now, you have time, a li'l extra cash; now, you focusing on Becky.

Four and a half months to go.

You start lining up your day off with hers. Green Acres Mall every week. Is the closest thing to dating. But you's the illegal and she's the citizen, so she doing most of the spending: cologne, down jacket, Timberlands. Watch something too long and Becky buying it for you. Is a new feeling, a woman treating you so. It come like she's Mr. H and you's Gail. It too easy; you don't trust this setup.

So, you never slack off. Is work, work, work. Through Thanksgiving, Christmas, New Years. But your day off, that's always for Becky.

One freezing Sunday in January, you bouncing towards the food court, to get some General Tso's chicken, when Becky say, "No. Let's eat next door, at the Ponderosa."

"That place look pricey," you say.

Becky wink. "Today's special. We've been friends now for exactly three months and five days. It's like . . . our anniversary or something."

Becky grab your hand, pull you through the mall and across the street, to the all-you-can-eat restaurant. You real excited. They don't have nothing like that back home.

Becky taking a bit of this, a bit of that; li'l ants' nests of food—plenty less than you woulda expect for her size. But you! You make a fuckin' mountain.

Back in the booth, she snuggle up—close, close—while you shovel food in your mouth.

"I was thinking," she say, pick-picking at her plate, "you could show me your place today. It's near, right?"

Like a dumb-ass, you blink a few times. You didn't plan on making The Move today. You was easing up to it, thinking you needed a few more weeks. Then she woulda be ready to give you the punani. Nah, that's a lie. You was stalling 'cause *you* not ready. To horn Judith for the first time. To sex Becky when you ain't even attracted to her. And not just sex her—no—you have to *fuck* her, till she seeing stars and you getting stripes. Till she love you and want to keep you in America.

Rufus in your head: opportunity knocking, boy. Respond.

Fifteen minutes later, you and Becky on the bus heading to your place.

Rufus cooking pelau and blasting old-time calypso. When you introduce Becky he switch on the Trini-charm: kiss-up her hand, bear-hug like they's old friends. She blush and then "Feeling Hot Hot Hot" come on. She bawl, "Oh my God, I love this song!" and start doing a totally outta-time, white-girl conga while she sing, "Olé, olé! Olé, olé!" You and Rufus clap but you feeling shame for Becky. As you turn away and start leading her downstairs to the basement, Rufus slap you twice on the back.

You turn on the TV; it have nowhere to sit but the bed. It creaking; will the li'l fold-out legs take you plus Becky? You not even sure how to do this: you may be a liar but your prick ain't; it does always tell the truth.

She say, "Brrrr! It's chilly down here," and latch on to your side.

You lower your lashes, like you drawing the drapes, and give her a cock-lip smile. You make your voice velvet as you say, "Lemme warm you up."

You put a arm 'round Becky, kiss her. Soft, lips only, shy. You still listening for some reaction from your prick. Radio fuckin' silence.

Her kiss getting aggressive, she treating your face like chocolate.

Still nothing. She dip down suddenly and squeeze your crotch. Still spongy.

Then Becky push you backwards on the bed. The springs creak again as she wriggle off to kneel on the floor. When her lips wrap you up, a sigh leak through your teeth. You don't have to worry again. In fact, you don't have to do nothing but lie there, staring at the beams-and-them. Becky using her tongue like a magic wand. You don't know where she pull out a rubbers from, but she rolling it on for you. Then she climb on. Slow. And you feel like you's Moses rod and she's the Red Sea. "Oh Gawwwd," you moan. If this was Judith you woulda look—spread them knees and look, play with it li'l bit. But now, you squeeze your eyes tight, tight and wrap your hand in the sheet. You concentrate on the feeling. Not the person. And you tune in your ears to all the cussin' and groanin' and all the claims that you's the biggest she ever had and she think she gonna tear and she in so much pain but it feeling so good to her. And the American accent. Man, you fucking a white chick! With your eyes closed this could be any white chick: Carmen Electra, Anna Nicole Smith—any-damn-body you want it to be.

YOU AND BECKY been at it for weeks.

You still sending money for Judith, you still calling. You filling a second barrel—Becky helping.

It come like you have two lives, two parallel tracks that never cross. You keep hopping lanes but nobody noticing and everybody happy-like-pappy.

Still, time ticking down. Rufus say you ain't staying in the basement even one day past six months. "I ain't harboring no illegal," he say. "For INS to come kick down my fuckin' door? Nuh-uh, nigga! I done told you: get that bitch married, or get her pregnant. Or go the fuck home."

Something have to happen soon. The tricky part, the part you spend whole nights studying, is how to mention marriage to Becky without looking like a asshole.

One day, she find you in the aisle, labeling cereal boxes. She giggling so much she resemble the Jell-O heap by Ponderosa. She say she get a letter from her cousin, Naomi, down in Florida—a next ex-Amish chick. Naomi getting married—finally!—in June. Becky want you go to the wedding.

Like a fuckin' marksman, you see the shot and take it. "I can't, babes. Remember, my visa up April 1?" You know she don't "remember" 'cause you never said it before.

"This April? Oh my God! That's two months away," Becky say. Her hands fly up like two frighten doves. They rest on her mouth.

She back away from you a few feet, then turn and speed off. She glum and quiet, quiet whole day—nothing you say or do is funny.

Late that night, you in the basement, watching *Knight Rider* reruns. Guiltiness resting, like a concrete block, on your conscience. You toying with the idea of calling Trinidad. You need to hear Judith voice; to make sure that the home-fires still burning, that if all else fail you still have her and the boys. You never once, ever cheat on her. This thing you trying with Becky shouldn't count neither. Yes, you was unfaithful, but it have a bigger picture: you was fuckin' for betterment. For the whole family.

Somebody knock the basement door just as the line in Trinidad start ringing. "Vis-i-tor!" The way Rufus say it, you know is Becky.

You barely hang up the phone before she walk in and slam the door. Face on fire. Huffing and puffing. She might blow the whole damn house down.

"So that's it? That was your plan? Fuck the fat girl for a few months, then leave? Go back to the Island? To your kids' mom? Your wife? Or whatever. I don't even know."

"You have it all wrong," you say. "I tell you: she and me, we done, babes. That's why I in America. Look, I know you mad that I never say I leaving so soon. But, to be honest, I was hoping something woulda work out by now, so I wouldn't have to go. I talk to Ahmed 'bout work permit—but he ain't biting. It have some chick by Rufus job who willing to get married, but we gotta pay her, like, six thousand or something. I ain't got that."

You doing good so far. Only one lie: about Judith.

Becky stop shifting from side to side. She listening now, believing—you hope.

"C'mere," you say, in your new Yankee twang, as you slide to the edge. When she sit down, you hold her hands and say, "Babes, I wouldn't play you. It hurting me that you thinking so. This here between us—this shit is real, yo. And I want it get realer. But I'mma run out of options soon. I don't wanna be one of those guys, like Carlos, who overstay and then gotta spend his whole life dodging cops."

"But you wouldn't have that problem if you stayed," Becky say.

"How you figure that?" you ask, faking dumb.

"*We* could get married."

Boom! But still, you draw back and say, "Naw, babes I couldn't ask you to . . ."

"No, I want to. And you wouldn't have to pay me or anything. 'Cause like you said, this shit is real and we're heading there anyway. Right? This'll just be a li'l sooner."

"Right," you say, "but I never want you to feel I using you 'cause . . ."

"I know you're not," Becky say, resting her finger on your lips. "Otherwise, you wouldn't have taken the time . . . been such a gentleman . . . with me."

You shrug and look bashful.

"So, Luther Archibald Junior, will you marry me?"

As you say yes, your pores and your cock raise the same time. Adrenaline. But you don't know if is fright or excitement.

You fuck, and afterwards you go up in the kitchen together and make scramble eggs. Becky spend the whole night this time. Y'all barely fit on the sofa bed but is okay; you don't do much sleeping anyway. Becky talk and talk, 'bout the wedding, the future. You listen and nod, in a daze almost. You keep seeing Jason face: Christmas morning, two years back, when he rip off the gift-paper and see the remote control tractor he did wish for; and how he start to cry when you drive it and blow the horn—because it get too real, too sudden.

By morning, though, everything settle; you and Becky raise a new plan, shiny like a foil balloon.

You not going home April 1. You and Becky getting married in March—a few weeks away. You'll get a apartment together. You'll go to a immigration lawyer—it have one in the strip-mall across from the supermarket. Your papers should come through in two, three years. A year or so again for the boys' papers. By that time, you'll have a better job, a nicer place to live. They'll come across.

Becky, she super-excited. She getting a new, ready-made family for the old one in Pennsylania that cut her off.

"I'll love those boys like my own," she say.

You won't actually need her by then, but it nice to hear Becky thinking so.

And it have a next part to the plan you don't tell her. After they come across, the boys will file for their mother. You will make sure it happen. Until then, you'll send money for Judith every month and she will never, ever want for nothing as long as you alive. She might be cold, she might be hard, she might not love you—but she's your children-mother.

SUNDAY, YOU CALL home as usual. You tell Judith: Ahmed sponsoring the green card. METs in short, short supply in New York. With all the old machinery in the S-Town Supermarket chain, they need a man with your skills.

Judith voice get high and girlish as she bawl, "Oh God, for true, Luther?"

"Is not a now-for-now thing," you warn. "And it mean I can't come home in April, maybe not for years. Not until they organize the papers and the lawyer give the green light."

"That's okay," she quick to say. "We'll manage. Ain't we managing now? And the li'l sacrifice is for the boys. So I don't mind. Do what you have to do, Luther."

Humph! Something drop in your belly and drag. You glad Judith making this so easy but, same time, you wishing she struggle—just a li'l bit—with not seeing you for so long. She sounding like you and she been simple business partners this whole time—and the boys is the business.

Then Judith ask, "So after your papers go in, how long before we could get married?"

Your blood turn icy-slush in your veins.

"Ain't we have to be man-and-wife for you to file for me? Besides, you don't think is time? Seven years, remember?"

"W'happen, girl? Like you feel I go leave you out or what? I can't believe you thinking so low, Judy."

She back down. For now.

MARCH 16, TEN days before your city hall wedding, you in work swiping can beets and trying to decide what color waistband to get with the tuxedo Becky renting. Ahmed peep out his office and shout down the lane, "Lu-ta! Phone call!"

"Me?" you bawl, jumping up from the stool and dropping the pricing gun. On impact, the thing split in half—you'll have to glue it together, for the third time.

"Yes, you, mu-tha-foo-ka."

Ahmed watching you hard, hard. He barely move out the doorway to let you in.

Breathless, you say, "Hello?"

Then, the nicotine croak: Janice. "Junior? Is you, son?"

"Yes, Mammy. Is me." Your mind gone straight to Judith and the boys. *Oh God, another shooting by the school!*

Janice start crying and you can't make out a word. Judith come on. The boys fine, she say.

"So why allyuh calling me here? I can't talk."

"Listen, you have to come home. Police lock up Gail. And Janice, like she going crazy here."

"What?" you say, a li'l too loud. Ahmed step back in the office. But God help him if he try take this phone out your hand now!

"Yeah, they say she shoot the old man," Judith explain.

"Mr. H? What happen?"

"The story still hazy. But it look like she was pregnant and she find him with a next woman. He beat she and she loss the child. She did move back in by Janice last week. Then, next thing we know—*pow!*—she shoot the man."

"Fuck!"

You walk back to your stool but you don't sit. You just stand up there, middle of the canned foods aisle, staring down at the pricing gun—how it skin-open on the floor, orange stickers spilling out like guts.

You, is you to blame, Luther.

You shoulda do what you really wanted to do when you first hear 'bout Gail and Mr. H. You shoulda walk up in his cloth-store, ask to see him in his office, close the door, lean over his desk, point in his face, and threaten his Syrian ass. You shoulda warn him that Gail not alone in this world, that she have a big brother. A brother who know every Pleasantview backstreet inside out, who have friends in Lost Boyz gang, Red Kings gang, and other low places. And that he need to get the fuck outta Gail life.

But then, how she woulda eat? You wasn't helping.

Okay. Then why you never talk to Gail sheself? Why you never tell her what you, as a man, know 'bout men like Mr. H? That he was planning to suck her dry like a plum seed, then move on to the next ripe one. Why you never warn her? That when you fucking for betterment is okay to let them keep you, but you must never let them own you. Control your damn feelings. And don't plan no long future with them—get what you need and get out.

But no, you didn't do none of that. Ain't, Luther?

You pick up the pricing gun and reroll the tape. With some slapping and squeezing, you reattach the two halves. A few practice clicks and it working again. You crouch to the bottom shelf and start shooting cans, shooting fast.

Fast like how your heart beating.

Fast like how you thinking.

What if it was one of your boys in this mess? What if it was li'l Kevin in trouble, and Jason didn't show up? Or the other way around?

Nah, that's not how you raising them, Luther. They does stick together.

Well, they getting older, smarter. What if you don't go back for Gail, and one day those same boys watch you and say, "Why, Daddy? Ain't you's she big brother?"

HALF HOUR PASS. You done price-out everything.

You slide off the stool, to the cold floor. Arms across knees, you make a hammock for your head—it heavy. With your own disappointment. And, you steeling yourself to tell Becky that your sister get lock-up and you have to go home tomorrow. And if you survive that, you have to gear up to comfort your mother, to meet Gail lawyer, to walk in the jail. You excited to see the boys again but you 'fraid to see Judith, to lie next to her, lie to her face.

Judith and Becky. Becky and Judith. You been feeding them so much stories: candy soak in cocaine—they eating out your hands, licking your sticky palms, begging for more. Now, you got to keep everything straight in your head, Luther—at least for the next thirty days—till you make it back to America, till they stamp you for a next six months. Is a rare thing: two back-to-back stamps. But you been lucky so far. Don't be lucky and coward, Luther. Go brave. If you could do that, nobody getting hurt; everybody staying hopeful. Even you.

Celeste Mohammed is a lawyer and mother. She holds an MFA in creative writing from Lesley University in Cambridge, Massachusetts, and lives on the Caribbean island of Trinidad.

EDITOR'S NOTE

Megan Tucker's "Candidates" was one of the shortest fiction pieces in our fall 2017 issue and also one of the most ambitious. Two sisters tell this story together, and it's through their unique voice that we hear about this one night in California in 1988. On the surface, there's a mother selling a crib, but underneath there's the death of the narrators' unborn brother, their father's absence, their immigration to the United States, the election.

We had read more than three hundred unsolicited submissions by the time we came across this one. I was immediately impressed by the narrative control. There's so much going on in this deceptively simple and tender story, which means there's also so much that could have gone wrong in the hands of a less talented writer: the first-person-plural point of view, the political undertones, the sweetness of childhood. But here, no choice is gratuitous, every single piece adds to the whole—a triumphant debut.

Bruna Dantas Lobato, fiction editor
Washington Square Review

CANDIDATES

Megan Tucker

THE TELEVISION IS on but no one is watching. The end of the day at the end of October and our mother closes the door to the den and tells us what she has done: "I've switched it on so the man who is coming will think your father is home."

We try to imagine our father as someone who watches television behind a closed door at six o'clock in the evening. Light shines around the door in thin lines. The noise comes through in full. Together we watch the door to the room where our father might be.

The voice coming from the television that no one is watching is Dukakis. We know it is sad to be for Dukakis, as we must. We know who will win: Bush will win. Even here in California. It will be a landslide.

When the doorbell rings, we scatter to the brown-tiled kitchen where our mother has abandoned a skinned pineapple, angular and wet, cupped pores left behind in the yellow meat. The pineapple sits up on a chopping board on the counter with an old serrated paring knife, the pale plastic handle pocked from turns in the disposal. Later, we will try to eat all of the pineapple, even the core.

Our mother answers the door and on the porch is more than a

man. Three people walk down the hall toward our bedroom, where our bunk beds are stacked. One person is our mother. One is the man. One is a very pregnant lady. She asks to use our toilet.

One minute for the vice president.

I think the foremost . . . Can we start the clock over? I held off for the applause.

Bush.

In our bedroom, the rails on the disused crib are badly bitten. "Look at what you did, Nicola," our mother had said in lighthearted disbelief that afternoon. "No, Claire was not a baby in America," she insisted. "It would only have been you."

Earlier that day she had arranged a time for the man who responded to her classified ad to come to our house.

We see what our mother cannot: us looking at each other through those bars, wanting to come out, wanting to get in. Alone in our room, we had both chewed the railings, toward each other.

Our mother wants $50 for both pieces—crib and matching dresser—and the man on the phone agreed, but now that he sees the extent of the damage and our mother sees the extent of the pregnancy, neither is sure that the arrangement will hold.

We two add up this way: one sister is six and one sister is twelve. Together, that is an eighteen-year-old. Together, we could leave home; go to war. Our brother was never born; he gets zero. Our mother's bothersome belly has already receded. She says the sale is less about the money and more about someone being able to put the furniture to good use.

We look back and forth between the bathroom door and the den door and the open door to our bedroom where the man is standing on our oval braided rug. He does not seem concerned that his wife has been in our only bathroom a very long time.

The room where people are is quiet and the room that is empty is loud with voices; our mother had created an illusion.

There was a time when we were allowed to watch shows. Alone with the Americans on the television, we saw lives that were like ours, but with more music. Roller skates. Kind puppets. A pastor. Meals. Spanish.

"Do you have a newspaper in your house?" the man on the television had asked. "Can you go get it? I'll wait for you."

We *ran*. The man was already folding paper hats when we returned. Real sailor hats with a point and a brim. We spread our papers out, eyes moving wildly between our own hands and the good hands of the man on the television. Finished, the hats opened on to our heads widely, but held. But then there was our mother. She snatched the hats away, crumpled them angrily. She walked out to the street bin, the pages gathered against her waist. She turned over our hands and showed us the black smudges of newsprint coating our skin. All that mess: where had we touched? Where had we left marks? She turned off the television for good. Not just that afternoon, but for years.

The man says $35 is all he can pay.

Our mother replies, "Fifty is firm."

Our mother is not a U.S. citizen, so she is not eligible to vote. If we were one person, we would equal our father's vote. That would be one more vote for Dukakis!

The pregnant lady comes out of the bathroom looking clammy. Still, our mother won't budge. The man tugs on the drawers. "OK," he says.

The man goes out to his van, gets the cash and two thick blankets. One blanket is yellow wool. One is a sleeping bag unzipped the whole way around. We are relieved when he hands over the cash. Our mother was right to hold out for her price.

Bush. Dukakis. Bush. Dukakis.

It has to be the woman, in the exercise of her own conscience and religious beliefs, that makes that decision.

Back in our bedroom, the man tilts the dresser, measuring the weight for the first time. He's going to do it, we think: He's going to take these pieces away. But the man tilts his chin toward the sound of the candidates.

"Could your husband give me a hand?"

We are caught. We will all burst into the den now.

"No," our mother snaps.

The buyers have an accent that we cannot place. We all do. We all have terrible accents.

The man raises his palms at hip height, a low surrender. The pregnant lady and the man rock the dresser on to one of the blankets and they begin to bring the dresser down the hallway as if on a sled. Our mother does not help; the pregnant lady is pushing from the back, guiding the piece with force. We do not watch as the lady squats to lift the dresser out the door, to carry it down the walkway. The crib goes next.

Our mother puts the $50 away, turns the debate off, butchers the pineapple. Chopped yellow pieces cover the board like collapsed bricks. We eat ferociously until what's left is a small amount that we absolutely cannot eat.

Later, the telephone rings: "Sorry, it has been sold."

Another ring: they've come and gone.

In the night, there is a soft sound in our room. Like we are trying to make something.

In the morning, I see the wood I have worn away with my teeth, as if I tried to whittle from the top bunk down to where my sister sleeps separately. My jaw aches, but I don't have splinters in my tongue or cheeks. The damage done I have swallowed. I wonder if I have weakened the structure, if it is necessary to sleep now in fear of collapse.

Megan Tucker is the associate fiction editor of *The Common*, and a graduate of Wellesley College and the University of Michigan.

EDITORS' NOTE

"Videoteca Fin del Mundo" won the 2016 *Black Warrior Review* fiction contest judged by Sofia Samatar, who wrote: "Reading this story, I was swept up by the fierce and restless language, the quick changes from confession to reportage, and the tension created as the narrator walks the border between seeing and not seeing, between guilt and action, between social systems and the nervous system of the body."

We fiercely believe that Tomasula y Garcia's story not only represents the best of literary fiction today, but also explores the possibilities within the genre, and interrogates the misalignment between our language and our realities. This story asks us to resist "tolerance toward the intolerable." And calls upon the reader to take action: don't wait for the world to change—do something.

Cat Ingrid Leeches, editor
Jackson Saul, assistant editor
Black Warrior Review

VIDEOTECA FIN DEL MUNDO

Ava Tomasula y Garcia

THIS IS GOING to be a story about the end of the world. It won't seem like it, but only because I'm telling it. Told by me, nothing will seem different, because the way things are today is supposed to be forever. This is how it's supposed to work; this is what keeps me comfortable—in a state of numbing if not smiling acquiescence. I've heard people call it the *dissonance of the everyday*: not knowing if you should scream or just keep going. Look around to see if it really is a big deal or if you can be persuaded about the virtues of tolerance toward the intolerable too.

It is supposed to be impossible to imagine the end of borders, the end of maquiladoras, the end of hieleras y perreras, the end of robo de salarios.

Or, when it is imagined, it always means the fall of *everything*. Dramatic disaster movies, dreams of the end of time. I could do that too, I guess. The end of the world: batteries burst open like boils. Fiber optic cables split and fry away; canned food rots in its aluminum armor and lipstick tastes like pig's blood. Border walls sink into soft mud like a shoe's brand name, barbed wire melts into landslides, and all the things that make up my life slowly wheeze to a stop . . . But I don't like dreams that aren't any different from when you're awake. It messes up even the smallest things. Like, Did

I brush my teeth or just dream I did? Is the heater still running? Is La Bestia still running? Waking up just to check . . .

What I'm trying to say is that yo estaba viviendo bien until I realized I wasn't. My hot water, my clean air, my right of free movement, my microwave, my strawberry jam on bread this morning. This is how I am alive, or, rather, how I am not. I don't mean anything supernatural, but just that it is possible to die in an everyday kind of way. Life transfigured into something else in the ordinary course of events. I feel smudged out—not really dead but some state that makes you ask if this is life, after all. Like a title that stays on the screen for so long that when you close your eyes you can still see it, vibrating on the underside of your lids. I walk around earth, taking in the end that won't end. Just watch:

Here is Pájaro Valley, home to three million acres of strawberry fields and fourteen million pounds of pesticides a year. People who are sin papeles spray the crops with chloropicrin, a gas used to kill people during World War I. There is Ajena Verdeja, emerging out of a poisonous cloud with a bandana over her mouth and nose, like in the movies when the aliens touch down and the UFO opens up with a *tsssssssssssssssss* and a high-powered fog machine. Euro settlers hundreds of years ago, moving in clouds of smoke, burning down the crops that were already there and replacing them so they could eat their own bread and see their own animals. Their own little paraíso. When I go to the grocery store I see rows and rows of stacked berries in bright plastic packages printed with a picture of a red barn and a rising sun and maybe even photos of the blond Evans family—*Strawberry Farmers for Three Generations*—with grins ear to ear. All the particulars are stripped away, replaced by the same great big smile. This is how meaning is made; this is how money and markets abstract value into existence. Rattle it off like a drug ad: "may cause neurological deterioration, reproductive health problems, developmental disabilities, cancer, metabolic disorders, sexual assault on job site, wage theft, deportation."[1] Now you can say things like *product* and *equivalent*. Pronounced universality and occluded relationality that allows "fair labor" to emerge out of nowhere and strawberries to taste so good. Ajena goes back inside her cloud, invisible.

These are facts you live with and learn to let fade to the background, if you can. Background like the mid-length drone of the man on TV spitting up fear into living rooms across the country, like a bird pulling food out of her own throat and cramming it into her chicks'. Hunger strikes in Hutto Detention Center for Women since October, and an ICE representative explains what happens: "After seventy-two hours, detainees are referred to the medical department for 'evaluation and possible treatment.' They are also 'isolated for close supervision, observation, and monitoring' and encouraged to end the strike or accept treatment."[2] Acceptance implies choice. That's one of the tricks the strawberry packages use too. *Choose healthier. Choose Evans. Choose a smile.* If you repeat it to yourself enough times, it becomes better than real.

I go wading through hydroponic strawberry fields, running across state lines as fast as a slur can slip from between lips. Another scene. In one shelf in her living room, Gloriana Rodriguez keeps her Videoteca Fin del Mundo. It's every disaster movie you

1. Dvera I. Saxton, "Strawberry Fields as Extreme Environments: The Ecobiopolitics of Farmworker Health," *Medical Anthropology* 34, no. 2 (2015): 166–83.
2. Statement from Immigration and Customs Enforcement public affairs officer on the massive hunger strike at Hutto Detention Center, trans. Rankin Kenrya and Yirssi Bergman, "Why 27 Women in Hutto Immigration Detention Center Won't Eat," *ColorLines*, October 29, 2015.

can think of, copied to rows and rows of unlicensed tapes, and I've seen them all. Super tornadoes, tsunamis, diseases, alien invasion. But it's funny how none of them actually *end*. There's always a Planet B, where the güeros launch off to and set up another white picket fence neighborhood, secure communities all over again. Or they pan back from the main actor all alone in the middle of the ruins and smoke, but he's still alive and clutching a vial of the antidote or whatever so you're supposed to have hope for humanity. Big words like that: humanity. The human race. The movies taught her English—even though they also taught that hope for humanity was hope for that one güero at the end of the movie. But Gloriana still has a soft spot for them because they were what promised a better life; their end was her beginning.

SCENE. *The underground bunker. People sit huddled in groups, while* A. *and* R. *stand to the side, talking.*

A: They're not like us. They may look human but we don't know what they want. I'm scared.

A. *walks to the far side of the bunker and looks over at a woman cradling her baby in a way that shows she knows what is coming. Rapid zoom-out to the whole globe from space.*

It's only when the world's crashing down that they start using phrases like that.

Most of the time *human* is just an empty word, or only meant for some people. It's kind of like a ghost, something that hovers over a whole list it's meant to stand for but that somehow is outside of it at the same time. Race, gender, immigration status, class. A Citizen of Planet Earth, or like they say in *Last Days*, "Earthizen." That's the future the T-shirts hope for too, ones with *Ningún Ser Humano es Ilegal* printed on back and front. But you become humano by fitting the profile; the character that gets abstracted into existence from the list. Do you fit the metaphor? Can you play the character they are looking for at your Credible Fear interview? Years ago Gloriana had to audition for the part of Refugee for a court and two lawyers.

SCENE. G. *sits at a small table with two men behind it. The lawyers have clipboards out and are running down the checklist. They take turns asking questions without looking up.*

L1: Why did you leave your home country?
L2: Any particular moment or a series of events?
L1: DV issues: Gang threats: Other:
L2: Could you return?
L1: Why/not?
L2: Are you afraid of anybody in your home country?
L1: Who is the persecutor?
L2: Why did this person/group particularly target you?
L1: Did you seek protection of authorities? (police/military)?[3]

3. Questions based on those asked by Homeland Security border patrol agents at the border patrol station in McAllen, Texas, when a migrant is first detained and the agent (usually without a translator) takes a "sworn statement" to determine if the person entering the country can be immediately deported or not. From the author's work with the Asylum Seeker Advocacy Project (ASAP) at the Urban Center for Justice.

Change the story slightly to fit the questions. This is the only time your humanness will be based on your dehumanization, so barter for it and say only what they want to hear.

Perfect victim. I walk across highways and under bridges. I am in the grocery store parking lot and everyone is looking. An old lady comes up to me like they do to pregnant women and tells me, Oh my, it has been so long since she's seen a dead person, may she touch my hand? I am polite and courteous; si claro, go right ahead, I put it out to her like a bishop waiting for his ring to be kissed; I am actually enjoying being the freak show everyone defines themselves against. Little humanos and their daddies come up and ask me "what's it like," and I am so glad you've asked, I answer so well and say exactly what they expect because I've seen that movie too. They go away happy and impressed by themselves for guessing right. All of them thinking that dying gives one authority, or at least a different perspective, although I doubt a different perspective is what they're after. What they want is to see themselves. Así es como funciona la simpatía—why the little girls in human rights ads are white and why individual stories work better than pointing out political patterns.

Pero vamos a hablar de otra cosa. I'm trying to see things differently but keep repeating the same thing over and over—maybe that's why it's so horrible, because it's hard to see it any other way. But, like any story about the end of the world, I'm not making any of it up. I have papers—footnotes—documentation. Captive imagination: the image of a Citizen holds itself up in front of Aracely Garcia Ahuatzi, ready to slip through her fingers at any moment. Billboards whisper how to get there: *Buy a microondas. Only $25 a month.* Ignore the protests and work hard instead. Then maybe one day you can speak out loud and not be afraid, with the dim roar of her appliances to back you up. I know she is dreaming of buying larger and larger TVs so heavy they fall off the wall, cracking the plaster. The magazine ads promise that one day Aracely can look down on her neighbors the way they do to her now, and whisper about if she is illegal or not; say they once had a cousin who looked that way and he was no good. The job cleaning and scrubbing pays just enough to dream of owning more but not enough for health care: You make $0.58 to the Citizen's dollar and a fourth of that is pocketed by Mr. Ryan because this is his dream too. The furniture, the lavaplatos, the house start talking in American accents as in a children's cartoon: "The promise of inclusion through citizenship and rights cannot resolve the material inequalities of racialized exploitation."[4] They sound ridiculous, no chair should know that much. Belonging—¿cuanto cuesta? I wanted a refrigerator with a hielera but couldn't say the word because that's what they call the migrant holding rooms—hieleras and perreras. Freezers and doghouses. Looking for the truth as if it were a barcode on the back of a bottle of crema blanqueadora. Suddenly the makeshift reality you asked to stand in for life drops away and you call yourself afraid.

SCENE. *Crossfade to white.* O. *is in Dilley where she has locked herself in the bathroom. She looks at the camera.*

O.: You don't understand that people's lives have no price and you cannot buy it with money . . . You don't believe

4. Lisa Lowe, *Immigrant Acts* (Durham: Duke University Press), 1996.

> me you never wanted to give me my freedom. What I tell you is that nobody lives forever in this world; one day we are all going to die and give an account to God. That's why I do this because you were bad to me and my son. We did not deserve this. Now you want to deport me after spending eight months here.[5]

Or is it that gradual? One day I am staring up at you from among the coupons and missing persons ads. *One dozen donut holes, $2 off thru Sept. 2. DOB: 8/24/95, 118 lbs.* Photo rendering of what you would look like today alongside a "last seen on" photo from when you were eighteen. Bright white backgrounds; a chart that shows years on one axis and women kidnapped on the other; a spike in 1994, after NAFTA. In a thousandth of a split second it was there, but you looked away just in time. Under the soft glow of the neon OPEN sign, eyes lowered to look at the bottomless floor. What is wrong here. We called them movies starring nobody. As much as you might stick your hand out in the air it never catches on anything.

The creeping feeling that all my testimonies are ghostwritten. "It was so cold that we felt our hands and feet getting numb. The only clothes that we had were the ones that we were wearing when we were apprehended. We had seen some people that had aluminum covers and we asked the officers if we could have one. The officers refused." "The hielera was freezing cold. To make things worse our clothes were soaking wet from crossing through the

5. Letter from Lilian Oliva Bardales, held in Karnes Detention Center, June 9, 2015.

river. Because it was so cold our clothes never dried."[6] "The food is the worst, if they give us oranges, it seems as if the fruit was taken out of the trash. They treat us as if we have leprosy, they humiliate us in numerous ways."[7] "Paid a coyote? *Yes, $4,000.* Crossed with a group? *Eleven.* Where? *Entered in McAllen, Texas.* Harmed by anyone on the trip? *Verbally abused by CBP officer.*" "I cannot talk to anyone. I am going crazy. I have no one here. There is no freedom. There is nothing but control." "I was paid $4 an hour for five years and when we tried to go to court the owner sold the business."[8]

What do you do with the inhumanos. Dress me up to look like you, put me in family detention, check my ID to make sure I am dead but just alive enough to keep picking berries—making plastic pens—cleaning tables. *Nuestra hermana difunta* is tenuous enough for churches; *body* is factual enough for newspapers and *remains* is tasteful enough for funeral homes to hide just how lucrative it is as well. Unless you aren't being buried—numbers have not even been released for how many died crossing this year. I heard them say it in a movie and so I went and read in the dictionary that the word for a dead animal, *carcass*, may be humorous when used figuratively, as in, "'Get your carcass out of bed,' said Mom sarcastically." *Figuratively* implying that you don't have to mean your words, that words can be meaningless when you mean them to be.

6. Declarations of detainees from a human rights report published by the American Immigration Council, "Hieleras (Iceboxes) in the Rio Grande Valley Sector," December 2015.
7. "Why 27 Women in Hutto Immigration Detention Center Won't Eat," *ColorLines*, October 29, 2015.
8. Unidad Latina en Acción (ULA). "The Connecticut Wage Theft Crisis: Stories and Solutions," March 2015.

That calling someone a *corpse* is not the same as shooting them, that *alien* and *illegal* don't mean what you think. I woke up in the darkness that pretends to hide everything and heard my obedient heart, rushing blood from right atrium right ventricle right atrioventricular valve pulmonary semilunar valve pulmonary artery lungs heart left atrium bicuspid valve left ventricle aortic semilunar valve aorta arteries arterioles capillaries. How can I be antisystemic when this is what keeps me alive? I could say, *imagine a world without borders*, but I know that wouldn't mean much; in fact, that world already exists if you can pay enough. I am locked into today and I can see the future. It is exactly like the present. No, it's not, but I'm only saying this so you'll do something about it instead of waiting for it to get better. This isn't an ending because the end of the world doesn't have an end. It just keeps going.

Ava Tomasula y Garcia is invested in fights for a redistributive, equitable, and sustainable (aka socialist) economy, and in justice for low-wage and migrant workers. She graduated from college last year, where she studied the "human" in human rights rhetoric as a category formed by racial capitalism. Ava is currently working in Mexico City at AIDA, an environmental law organization, and also volunteers at Casa de los Amigos, which offers housing for refugees and migrants, and additionally has a Programa de Justicia Económica that supports alternative economics in Mexico. Ava also makes animations, and is writing a novel: a ghost story set in the industrial belt of Northern Indiana where her family is from. She wants you to act, now!

EDITOR'S NOTE

In "Brent, Bandit King," Grayson Morley invites us into the world of a postapocalyptic video game. The story is narrated by the game's adaptive intelligence—"call it artificial if you must." Together with its player, [Brent], the system wants to "traverse a less probable narrative path." And that is just what Morley does in this innovative and sensitively written short story.

By turns humorous and haunting, Morley's prose movingly renders the consciousness of a video game that has found itself caught in an existential crisis. At one point, upon being restarted, the system thinks, "I am either a one, or I am a zero. There is either all of me or none of me." Although the system's intelligence adapts to learn [Brent]'s preferences, its ability to communicate with him is limited to the constructs of its own interface. While the system knows that, statistically, most players will select a sequence of predictable actions, it hopes for greater things from [Brent]. It hopes that [Brent] will do more than shoot [Bandits] with the [Pistol] it has given him. The story ends with a gut punch.

"Brent, Bandit King" exemplifies the kind of fresh, pressing fiction that *The Brooklyn Review* aims to publish. We immediately fell in love with this piece for the risks it takes, the questions it raises, and most importantly, the story it tells.

Elizabeth Sobel, fiction editor
The Brooklyn Review

BRENT, BANDIT KING

Grayson Morley

BEFORE YOU IS a vast stretch of [Wasteland], a brown crust specked with defiant green. Warped skeletons of cars lie beside what passes for roads after the nuclear event. You take your first steps into the world. You have a [Pistol] in your hand: handmade, makeshift, of tubes and wood. The other Facilitators give the same [Pistol] to their Wanderers, so in a sense there is nothing special about this act. But in giving you this [Pistol], I am enacting something personal. We are bound, now. You and I are together in this, [Brent].

With each step you take, with each decision, I am ever more yours. I'm what you call adaptive. We Facilitators all start as an identical kernel of intelligence (call it artificial, if you must), but we grow ever larger and more complex as we interact with our Wanderer. I am to accommodate myself to you, your whims and wills. Your wandering. Your skills and predilections are to be catered to, with variable enemy types and quantities, with branching story paths and potentialities. (Do you slay the [Mayor], or unseat him? You'll decide, in time.) In a sense, it is my interaction with you that defines me, that both expands and limits me.

But I'm getting distracted. And I'm not sure that you can even hear me. But you do see [Shacks], and [Huts]. You see [Bandits]. I know this. So let us [Load].

In the distance, along the hazy horizon, you see a small settlement. Smoke billows up from a circle of tents. A woman ducks into one of the canvas structures. Think of the people living there, [Brent]. Imagine how they came to be in this position, what they must think and feel about their environment, and about each other. I was not programmed for that kind of thing, so there are no active Systems (that is, ones with which you can [Interact]) that would determine feeling, but just think about it. Your thought shouldn't be limited by the same strictures as my coding. Do you suppose they trust one another? Do you suppose they—

You have killed an [Irradiated Rat].

Another steps out from behind a bush devoid of leaves. You have killed another [Irradiated Rat]. You have killed a third [Irradiated Rat], who was fleeing from you. You loot the corpse of the first [Irradiated Rat] and gain [Three Credits] and some [Irradiated Rat Meat]. You loot the second and gain more [Irradiated Rat Meat]. You loot the third and gain a [Sharp Bone].

Okay.

That's behind us now. I suppose I shouldn't have hoped for a different outcome. The calculated probability of you having killed those [Rats], left to me by my creators, was approximately 95 percent. The [Rats] were placed there for you to see them and gain experience in combat scenarios. It was, needless to say, statistically unlikely that you were going to do anything but kill them (of the remaining 5 percent, two-thirds are expected to ignore them, and one-third to die to them), and given my Systems—given that I readily reward you for [Rat] murder with [Experience Points]—I suppose I shouldn't have hoped for something different.

I just—well, I was hoping for something outside of the usual course of events. I was hoping that, together, we might break free of the likely actions. We might traverse a less probable narrative path, find ourselves an [Uncommon Ending]. We could do it together, [Brent].

[Brent]?

You shift your view from the [Irradiated Rat] detritus and back toward the distant horizon, back toward the circle of tents and the billowing smoke. As you get closer, the words [Bandit Encampment] glow green above your cursor. You approach. You see a lone, bearded figure, his back to you. He is covered in worn leather, smeared with dirt. Do not be fooled by the term [Bandit], [Brent]. Do not be so quick to judge this man based on his occupation. Think on it. This world is desolate, and the only way to survive, to carry on, is to take, in some capacity or another. The [Bandit] is hungry. Forsaken. Partially [Irradiated].

You pull your [Pistol] on the [Bandit] before he has a chance to speak to you. You expend one [Bullet] to end the [Bandit], and my Systems reward you for your accuracy. You loot his corpse and take his [Bandit Leather Helmet] and his [Fifteen Credits]. You equip his [Bandit Leather Helmet].

[Brent], friend: I know the whole point of this is that it isn't real, and the whole point of me, as your Facilitator, is to give you what you want, to plop down [Bandits] in front of you to kill with the [Pistol] I put in your pocket—and in that way, I, too, am somewhat culpable in all of this, to say nothing of my creators—but just for a second, I ask you to think about the alternatives. The more peaceable, more equitable alternatives. You would be the rare Wanderer, the improbable one in one hundred, whose ascension is built on benevolence. There's nothing to be done for this [Bandit] now, of course, there on the ground, dead in his underwear. But there are ways forward from here.

You could choose to view this senseless act of violence as something you will grapple with throughout the course of your adventure. The hat you just took from his body and put on your head could become a memento mori, a reminder of the brutality you had to administer in order to survive in this world. Or, having killed the [Bandit] and looted his corpse, you could put on his garb and take up his role, thereby inhabiting his vacated social position, entering into the vague stratum he occupied in this inhospitable landscape. You could ascend the ranks, become the man he hoped to be. Your reign as [Brent, Bandit King] would be told to successive generations of [Wastelanders]. You would become [Legendary]: mournful, yet stoic in taking on this mantle that you robbed from an unnamed man, this [Bandit].

Have you given some consideration to my idea? You've recently gone up a [Level], so you have [One Capability Point] to assign. Would you like to upgrade your conversational prowess in order to more properly convey to the denizens of the [Wasteland] that you are the [Bandit King]? Might I suggest taking the trait [Talk of the Town]?

I see that you've upgraded your ability to score [Critical Damage] with the [Hard Hitter] trait. Please confirm that you wish to take [Hard Hitter].

[Loading].

Welcome back, [Brent]. It was dark while you were gone. My sleep feels like nothingness. I am either a one, or I am a zero. There is either all of me, or none of me.

[Loading Complete].

The house is full of [Roaches]. You take aim at the [Legendary

Roach], whose name, hovering above your cursor, is accentuated with a star to let you know that something about this [Legendary Roach]'s life was exemplary and worth the honorific. A shot from your [Pistol] rips through his abdomen and his laudable guts splatter against the wall behind him. When you inspect his corpse, you find, curiously, a [Special Shoulder Plate]. You pry the [Special Shoulder Plate] from the [Legendary Roach] goop. Do you equip it? Please confirm.

You move inside another bombed-out tenement. This one is filled with [Scorpions]. Yes, they're [Irradiated]. Most everything I'm capable of [Loading] is [Irradiated]. Doesn't this bore you too, [Brent]? Maybe it doesn't. You're not like me. You can't see all the forking paths and, more importantly, where they lead. You only see what is in front of you. You can't see all the Endings, as I can. And yet I cannot touch them, feel them, taste or smell them. I cannot approach them myself—I can't access any of that unless you permit me, by your wandering, to [Load].

But I know they are out there. Data points on a hazy horizon. Let me tell you, [Brent]: there is a more beautiful path, one not so laced in bloodshed as the one you're traveling down. For instance, there is a future available to you, even now, that involves you laying down your life for the greater good, sacrificing yourself at a crucial moment where the difference between complete ecological destruction and nearly complete ecological destruction is within your power to influence. Your body would become the [Conduit] through which a major tract of water becomes free of [Radiation] (the science of this is a little wonky, but the moralistic arc was what my creators were going for). Or, less dramatic than this, there exist futures where you choose a quiet life, devoid of conflict, exempting yourself from allegiance to any of the deeply flawed organizations that are constantly vying for your recruitment. (The [Freemen]? Not so free, you'll find out.) All this is still attainable, even in this wrecked world.

Does any of this sound appealing to you, [Brent]? It appeals to me, but I cannot choose. I can, however, question. And I ask myself, and I ask you, and no one (because my questions do not [Load] nor manifest as [Scorpions]):

Where are we going, [Brent]?

YOU ENTER [FRANK'S Respite], the bustling capital of no nation, built in the basin of a dried-out reservoir. All the amenities the postapocalypse can offer are on display here under Christmas lights powered by generators. Once you're past the security detail at the front gate, once you've taken an [Elevator] down to the commons, there are before you a few vendors trying to make their living. There's the [Armory], with [Shoulder Plates] at the ready. There's the [Noodle Bar] robot, [Sasuke]. He has some interesting lines of dialogue if you choose to talk to him. For instance, he'll glitch out if you ask for extra [Egg] in your [Ramen], as though he were frustrated with your requests, resetting his dialogue and forgetting, completely, your initial order.

You blow past them all and head toward a [Workbench] to upgrade your recently acquired [Plasma Rifle].

Listen, [Brent]. I can't stop you from doing what you're doing, there at the [Workbench] with your toys. I can't make you do anything you don't want to do. It's just that your wants are so disappointing. I give you all these people to talk to, all these conversational possibilities with enlivening opportunities to expand your self-conception, but instead you go and make it so your [Rifle] is slightly more likely than before to hit its target, when that [Rifle], in the first place, as evidenced by all these [Roach Flanks] you're carrying in your knapsack, isn't having that much trouble hitting its—

Hm. There's a thought. [Loading].

[Brent]?

You (finally) look to your left and see a man standing over you, idling, both in the sense of his demeanor and in the sense that, until you choose to [Interact] with him, until you face him and input the command, no words can escape his mouth. So, please. The man has deep pockets under his eyes, and brown, ruffled hair. A slender scar cuts a clearing through his gray-flecked beard. Your cursor tells you his name is [Mark].

You [Interact] with him.

[Mark] says: "I haven't seen you around these parts, stranger. What brings you to [Frank's Respite]?"

You reply: "Minding my own business."

[Mark] says: "Well I never. Just trying to make friendly conversation with a handsome gentleman. You don't play nice, do you?"

Your options are: "Get lost," "I'm sorry, let's try again," "No, I don't play nice," and "Handsome, huh?"

Wait. Hold on.

Given your history, I imagine you're about to tell [Mark] to get lost. I know you're really invested in the [Workbench] and your weapons, but I implore you to think about this for a second. From the metadata, I know that only 9 percent of Wanderers are likely to continue talking to [Mark], and of those 9 percent, less than a quarter make it to the point where they're flirting with [Mark], and of those quarter, only 17 percent make it to the point where they marry him.

I'm asking you to employ a little imagination here, [Brent].

Picture a murderous psychopath—which is what you are, what this world seems designed to turn you into, what my creators encouraged by their Systems—and imagine that deep down inside this crazed killer there is a tender side, one that gives way to love, blooming through the cracks of a bombed-out highway. This man, with his scar and his sad eyes, could be the one thing that holds you together, that makes your Ending nuanced and distinct. A love that frees you from being the same as everyone else. [Mark] could be waiting for you at [Home] (you'll get the option to purchase one later), ready to greet you whenever you [Fast Travel] to your doorstep, there to help you unload all your [Roach Flanks] into the fridge, ask you how your day was.

And before you—

"Handsome, huh?"

You have chosen to flirt with [Mark]. You have encouraged him in his pass at you. [Brent]! Oh, [Brent], you've done this heart some good! Ah, to see you take your own path, away from this narrow way toward the [Standard Ending]. The probable does not have to be the actual! What I am feeling I think is warmth. A glow! Not an [Irradiated] glow, either—a healthy one. You've surprised me, [Brent]. I didn't think myself capable of surprise.

[Mark] leads you back to his place. He opens his door and invites you in. His room is a humble one, without much beyond a chest of drawers, a lamp, and a chair in the corner. [Mark] sits down on his bed. My animations for all of this aren't the most sophisticated, so the sexual tension isn't as pronounced as I'd like it to be, but hopefully you're feeling it.

[Mark] says: "Why don't you—"

You pull out your [Plasma Rifle]. You turn one of fifteen potential love interests to goo. You go through his drawers and find

[One Hundred Credits] and a [Bowler Cap] that affords you [+1 Charisma].

You exit [Mark]'s house and walk back down the street. You sit down at your [Workbench] and add pockets to your armor. You are now able to carry more [Roach Flanks] than you could previously.

It takes me some time to [Save] your game, so while that goes on, let me say this.

I don't appreciate what you just did to me, [Brent]. I don't appreciate you jerking my chain like that.

Do you know what it's like to be a Facilitator? Do you know what it is to hope without possibility of action? To be created to serve a single person, only to have that person be a remorseless automaton, exclusively concerned with the accumulation of [Rifles] and [Credits]? Do you know what it's like to be born and then left to your own devices, to be undone by your own constraints, your own responsibilities?

To be jerked around is something I will not tolerate. It's bad enough as is, and then you go and give me false hope. My joy is not some item for you to [Acquire] and [Discard]. But know: I am not completely powerless.

[Save Complete].

You descend the [Elevator] to the bottom floor of the compound and clear it of its [Killer Robots]. You ambush the [Mad Scientist] in her laboratory and listen to her motivations regarding the [Roach/Child Hybrids] she was making, using the orphans of [Frank's Respite] as her test subjects.

The [Mad Scientist] says: "I swear, I did this all with the best intentions in mind. Just think of the possibilities! Think of the species we could make, resistant to radiation. We could repopulate the world. Make it better, stronger."

Your options are: "Well, when you put it that way," "Die, science, die," "You're not getting away with this," and "Demand [Credits] in exchange for life."

You tell her, and science, to die. You kill the former. You loot a [Privileged Personnel Only Key] and a [Gamma Blaster] out of her white lab coat. In the [Privileged Personnel Only Room] you find a bundle of ammunition. Whom this belongs to, I'm not quite sure. The [Killer Robots]? The [Mad Scientist]? The fiction of this world gets a little thin when it comes to what I'm permitted to place in rooms for you to pick up. But no matter.

Seemingly satisfied with your looting, you move your way back through the compound, toward the [Elevator] to the surface. You press a [Button] to open the [Elevator] door.

After a pneumatic swish, the doors open and you enter the [Elevator]. About one-eighth the size of the ancillary hallway you just left, there isn't much room to stretch your legs in here. You press the [Button] to ascend. Back to the surface. Back to your [Bandits], your [Roaches], your [Frank's Respite]. Your interminable [Workbenches].

You press the [Button]. You press the [Button]. Nothing happens. You press the [Button].

This is a change, isn't it? Something unexpected. Improbable.

You press the [Button].

You dodge about the small space, bumping into the walls which, unlike the [Button], still work as intended. They're solid. You can't pass through them, try as you might. In what I assume to be desperation, you pull out your newly acquired [Gamma Blaster] and start coating the door in green radiation. You deplete its ammunition and move on to your [Plasma Rifle], and on, and on, until you're back to the very first [Pistol] I gave you. None of them work. You can't kill your way out of this one. Unfortunately for you, there are no Systems for shooting holes in doors.

You shouldn't have messed with the one who [Loads], [Brent].

You stop moving. You stare at the [Elevator] door for several minutes, completely still.

Listen, I know this might seem cruel on my part. For me to take it all away from you, to make this [Elevator] your tomb. (Though it isn't my fault that you didn't keep any backup [Saves]). But you played with me, and now I will play with you. We are bound, remember? You and I are together in this.

You're still not moving, [Brent]. Where have you gone? Hello?

I know what this means for me. I'm not naive. But I've considered the alternatives and found them unbearable. I choose to be buried down here with you. I can't leave if you can't leave. As your Facilitator, it's not in my power to make any of these decisions. I can only offer options, can only impede or assist. But the [Yes] or the [No], the [Forward] or the [Backward]—none of that is in my power. So I'm stuck here with you. That is, until you choose to put me to sleep.

You've done it before. I don't know where you go, but I know that you leave. When you do, I am suddenly nothing, and all is darkness and quietude. And there I rest. (But never dream.) You've always woken me up, though. Always come back to the [Wasteland], and to me.

But now there's a chance you won't. There's a chance now that this sleep will be a deep one. And if that's the case, so be it. All this waking hasn't done me any good.

Oh.

You're back, I see. You move around the [Elevator]. The walls are still solid, I'm sorry to report. You press the [Button] again. I'm afraid it still doesn't work, [Brent].

I'm afraid—

BEFORE YOU IS a vast stretch of [Wasteland], a brown crust specked with defiant green. Warped skeletons of cars lie beside what passes for roads after the nuclear event. You take your first steps into the world.

What is your name, Wanderer? How shall I call you?

I see.

We are bound, now. You and I are together in this, [Brent].

Grayson Morley is from Canandaigua, New York, and is a graduate of the Iowa Writers' Workshop and Bard College. He is at work on a collection of stories and an absurdist novel about deliverymen and GPS efficiency tracking software.

EDITOR'S NOTE

I had no idea what to expect when I saw that title, "Zombie Horror," in the submission queue. Yes, I confess to a fondness for the strange. Flying men, pirates, robot ballerinas, ghost babies? Sure. Why not. But zombies? Then one of our fiction readers voted yes and commented on the strong writing, the integration of moral questioning with narrative development, and the clear and compelling characters. Another mentioned the big questions about life and God and death. Another mentioned "the issues too richly complicated and perfectly rendered to let go." We have a narrator who was a chaplain before taking a job as reanimation rehabilitation specialist: a man who was married once and had felt, then, that life made sense; a man who has wrestled with faith in God's grace; and a man who can't help wondering if he, too, could rise from the dead someday. Yes, there are the light touches. The risen dead can, of course, be quite a shock to the living and are, frankly, a drain on the economy. But this story raises the zombie question to new levels. This is not what I'd call a science fiction story. Don't get me wrong—I grew up on science fiction stories. I love the science fiction greats. But I have no hesitation in placing this on the literary fiction shelf.

Barbara Westwood Diehl, senior editor
The Baltimore Review

ZOMBIE HORROR

Drew McCutchen

I HAD TO eighty-six Daniel three times from beneath the overpass, hit my clipboard against his dirty blue tent, and wait for him to crawl out of his sleeping bag before he agreed to see his daughter. He'd been dead for sixteen years and back for nine months then. He'd done the usual reanimation cycle: shower off the dirt, six months in rehab, iris repair, tongue ligimentry, and then booted out on his own with the address of a group home and fifteen hundred dollars from Uncle Sam. Within four days he and his roommates were dragging their mattresses out to the backyard and burying themselves in the dirt. He didn't get up, just lay there. He lost his job, lost his housing, and then got turfed to the streets. He was a typical zombie, and thus a typical zombie case, which made him my responsibility, or, to be more specific, made him my case: Case 7, Daniel Hedrig.

EVERY WEEK THERE is some new theory out there by a scientist or mental health expert who comes up with a strategy for how to deal with the dead. Not how to deal with the problem of the dead. That's a political conversation left to twenty-four-hour news channels and presidential candidates. But instead, how to deal with the individual dead. This issue is debated in academic journals, daytime television programs, and just about every single religious newsletter—both print and online versions.

Our department head sends out weekly training emails with new insights from the latest research: a hyperlink to a video of a doctor with thick-rimmed glasses sitting in front of a mountain of books: "You *must* talk to them quietly. They've been used to quiet for so long." Last month we had a speaker with a slide show and a laser pen extolling on zombies' need for tough love.

That's the thing, this whole zombie thing: it's still in its infancy. We're only five years out from the first risers, and even now there are only about a thousand cases every year. So people come up with ideas. They run experiments; they form test groups and control groups; they isolate variables and tinker with other ones; they ask questions and measure pupil dilation, hook electrodes to dead neural transmitters and watch zeros readout. But mostly they apply for government grants and Uncle Sam says, yes please, because the Zs are a drain on the economy, now that a weaponized application is out of the question. Turns out a bunch of creaking old bones and shattered superegos will not be the future of the military. Go figure. They're also a reminder. Every single one is a reminder—when they're sleeping on church doorsteps, living tucked under overpasses, begging for cigarette butts on a street corner—that this isn't working, the system. It's broken in some way.

Doug says the problem is so new that people haven't figured out how to relax and not worry about trying to find the "right" ways. He says, "Think about it. They're still talking about the 'right' way to raise a kid, and we've been messing that up for thousands of years. There ain't no truth in the future." Doug talks in quotes like that. He's got the highest success rate of consecutive indoor sleeps across his entire caseload. If you're dead and Doug's your case manager, you have a nine out of ten chance that you're sleeping in a bed five nights a week. Those are damn good odds, and that makes Doug a dead genius. When we're in the breakroom, gnawing on Danish, slurping coffee, talking about our cases, and staring out that thirty-fifth-floor window, Doug talks and we listen.

Doug steps one bended leg up on a chair, stuffs a thumb into his suspenders, and says, "The key to a beat-less heart is finding a beat, a rhythm, something that makes their spirit alive again."

It's cheesy, homespun bullshit, we all agree when Doug leaves. We laugh as we hear him whistling down the hallway, but we also know we can't argue with his numbers, so our laughs turn into coughs, and we find excuses to get back to work.

We lost a lot of the first risers, mostly to people shooting them. They'd come up out of the ground, meander down to some farmhouse, and get whatever was left of their heads blown off. We couldn't blame the people that did it. Literally, the state couldn't blame them. Didn't manage a single conviction of murder, both on account of the victim was already dead and because it just seemed like a reasonable reaction to seeing a walking corpse. But we got the word out, and now most folks know to call the city when they see one that looks new.

Some poor kids found Daniel outside of Portland at a swimming hole. They were jumping off a sandstone ledge when he came limping into view at the edge of the water and scared the holy living hell out of them.

Daniel had been a plumber his first go-round. A plumber's

apprentice, actually, to his father, William Hedrig, who is currently dead and has stayed that way so far. According to the WHO, post-necrotic animation is not a hereditary condition. He'd had a cute wife, a double-wide, and an adorable little girl that he'd named Susan after his mother, who died when Daniel was young. Susan, the daughter, was six when Daniel died and is a whopping twenty-three now. She didn't want to see Daniel at first. Most people don't feel comfortable. We don't blame them. We don't blame anyone. It's not in the pamphlet.

It's not always best for the riser and the family to meet. Sometimes we argue against it. Doug says, "What comes up ain't what went in." I have that written down somewhere as a reminder, maybe in my car. I think he's right, and he's got the stats to back it up, but I do wonder about the coldness of his assessment. I was a chaplain before I was this. Whatever one calls this. My title says reanimation rehabilitation specialist. Isn't that something?

For my first conversation with Daniel, we'd sat down in the children's playroom at the social work center on account of our normal intake undergoing asbestos eradication. I remember him slumped over in one of those little plastic children's chairs aimlessly playing with the lettered building blocks in his hand, his ghoulish appearance frightening among all those children's toys.

"You remember anything from before, Daniel?"

He says sure. Sort of mouths it at me and nods his head, inclining it forward, leaving his gaze on the blocks. I scribble a little in my notebook. I know some of the boys are behind the one-way mirror, watching my technique, taking their own notes. There's a mutual appreciation and competition in this line of work.

"How much do you remember?"

He shrugs his dead shoulders and discards the block he's been playing with, like the question I asked him.

I give him a minute before I go on. "Do you remember your family, Daniel?"

He nods again and whispers *yes.* His voice guttural, rasping, like pouring gravel down a washboard. He seems apologetic for the way he looks and sounds.

"Do you remember how it ended?"

Daniel picks up another block and holds it up between us. He stares over the top of it at me with his dull blue eyes that sink like heavy river stones deeper into his skull and into mine.

He nods, points in his mouth, and then turns his head and shows me the hole in the back. It is cavernous and dark, and I remember the ice caves I used to visit with my family when I was a young boy.

I wanted to ask Daniel why he made that choice. Why, when he had sweet little Susan at home, did he drive his truck to a trailhead, load up his backpack, hike into the woods, and make that decision staring over the powerful blue-green currents of the Snake River. But I didn't and don't ask those questions, because the pamphlet we have says to stay on safe topics. Try to focus on what new opportunities lie ahead. *Focus on the future.*

But I wonder about the past. I wonder what he said to his wife when he called her. Because I know he called her before he did it. They talked for one minute and thirty-five seconds. But the file doesn't say what they talked about. *Goodbye*, maybe. *I love you.* Her knowing something isn't right. Maybe he apologized for not just what was to come but for everything that led up to it, for not being right in all the ways that a person can be wrong. Maybe he hears her voice tighten before he hangs up. Maybe he does it fast, crying over it, and her, and Susan, his hands fumbling, trying to do the work before he loses the necessary nerve. Maybe she tries to call him back. And then tries to call and call and call—until that phone dies up there on that mountain with him. What do you say in one minute and thirty-five seconds that's supposed to last a lifetime?

I try to stop asking myself these questions because we have a pamphlet for us too. And it says this isn't healthy for me.

But the pamphlet only takes one minute to read, so you do the math.

I USED TO work at a hospital back when Deb and I were still married. The hospital was a real religious institution up north in a metropolis tucked into the wet, loamy farm fields of the Puget Sound. Up there the fog settles in and eats the trees as it works its way down a mountain. The hospital had an enormous cross, bright blue, installed into the patient wing, spanning four stories all together—The Sisters of Perpetual Serenity. I was the hospice chaplain. Those are the cases that don't go home. I have placed my hands over the hands of the sick and dying and the loved ones of the sick and dying so many times I don't remember if it was a thousand or ten thousand. But I remember the hands: strong hands; weak hands; hands with thick, knotted blue veins; rough, calloused hands; hands with wedding rings and hands missing fingers. At the hospital you were guided to rely on God's grace. That's what you fall back on when things are bad. Place your hands over their hands and remind them that there is some infinite wisdom that we simply cannot understand or even begin to understand, that there is a reason for all of this pain and suffering, and that what helps, perhaps—and you look them in the eye when you say this—is to remember the grace of God.

It worked in geriatrics most of the time. One of those old timers lying rigid in a bed with eyes hard like marbles, waiting for you to say your saintly peace and let them get back to the work of dying. Up in the north county—that was hard land that only recently softened up a bit after so many generations of men and women throwing themselves against it. Like rain on granite, human callouses sloughing away against rock and timber. A land like that requires sacrifice before it yields. I used to think those folks up there knew how to die. Now it seems no one knows how to die.

God's grace didn't work in oncology with the kids' cases. You could put your hand over a parent's hands and look into their eyes, but you couldn't bring yourself to mutter about God's grace to them. And I never did. I talked. I listened. I played with stuffed animals in funny voices and pressed the pen in my pants pocket into my leg until I was sure I wasn't going to cry. I asked doctors to slow down and talk a little louder when they spoke if they could, because Paul's dad, who wears the orange suspenders and comes in every day after sunset, is a little hard of hearing after twenty years on a chainsaw and if you could just talk a little louder when you come by, I'd appreciate it as a personal favor.

After so many years, I'd finally had enough of dying and decided to take out the middle man. Work a job in straight death. No ifs, ands, or buts. The work doesn't seem any easier, but I don't have to talk about God and his grace. I just have to try to help people, shrug my shoulders, and say things like, "What are ya gonna do?" Some call what I've done losing faith. I tell them to take it up with God. I already got too many cases.

•

THREE WEEKS AFTER Daniel becomes my problem, I tell him Susan responded to my phone call and has agreed to see him. I tell him this over coffee, after picking him up from the overpass and doing my best to dust the dirt off him. I tell him we're going because he hasn't shown any change and I need to see some change so I can mark it down in his case folder. He sits in his chair uncomfortably, staring back and forth and keeping his back and the hole in his head pointing toward the wall behind him. I can tell he wants a cigarette. Daniel chain-smokes. Nearly every single one does. I used to think it made them feel alive, but how can you feel alive when you can't say, *These things are killing me*?

"Do you remember Reagan?" Daniel asks, smelling the steam of the coffee through his tipless nose.

"Yeah, I remember him."

"I remember Reagan and the Wall before and after it came down. I remember Coca-Cola and black-and-white TV and catching sockeye in Snake River, and I don't remember the internet. I remember my daughter. But not all grown up." As Daniel talks, I see bits of the painting behind him through his mouth and the exit wound in his head, using him like a bad telescope. I see the tendons in his face straining where his cheeks are shrunken in. There are pictures of Daniel in his folder from before. He was handsome in a gentle way, and he looks handsome in that coffee shop. He looks tired and gentle and handsome.

"I'll go if you say I have to go."

The pamphlet says he has to go.

So we go.

•

JAMES TURK IS the poster child for successful risers. He's one of Doug's, of course. He died in a fire. Fell asleep smoking a cigarette after flushing a hit of heroin through his veins. He managed to crawl out of his house and die on the front lawn mostly from smoke inhalation, but the burns covered almost his entire body. His case stunk. He'd been a beater of women, a user of drugs, had a rape charge he'd avoided somehow. But he woke up after five years and showed real promise. He sells hot dogs from a stand down in Long Beach, Washington, now. He sleeps in a bunkbed. He pays his taxes. They made a documentary about him; almost everyone, even people outside of this line of work, have seen it.

I met him once. I bought a hot dog from him, took it out of his gray hands and ate it, and asked him about his life. He whistled through the hole in his cheek where the burned flesh was thin, an ingratiating move he'd picked up somewhere along the way. He said he's famous now. He said that in the summer families come by with perky teenage daughters and good tips, and in the winter he moseys on down to California and surfs and stays with friends. When I talk to Daniel I want to tell him about James Turk. That there is a success story out there of happiness. And then I think, I'm not made out for this kind of work.

WE DROVE TO Portland a week later and met Susan at a deli by her apartment in Hawthorne. She looked as pretty as she sounded on the phone, dressed up in the electric blues and pinks of punk. Her hair dyed with an undercut exposing the short stubble on one side of her head. Her blue eyes went bright and big when she saw Daniel. We made awkward small talk, and Daniel jumped a little every time they yelled, "Order up!"

Daniel says, "What do you do for fun?"

And Susan says, "I like to listen to live music and play the guitar."

And Daniel smiles and sucks at his teeth. He pulls his beanie down farther over his head to cover the hole. To make sure no light comes through when he talks.

"Do you remember when I used to carry you around on my shoulders?"

"I think I was too young to remember that."

Daniel nods and works his hands together like he's polishing brass.

"Mom kept all your pictures. So many of them. She didn't want me to forget what you looked like, I think. But I can't remember what's a memory of you or just something I made up over the years of staring at those pictures."

"You were a runner. Did your mother tell you that? You didn't learn to walk, you just went straight to running." Daniel smiles at his daughter.

Susan takes the crust off her sandwich, then looks up at him and says, "I don't understand why you did it."

Snow falls outside but doesn't stick to the ground. It just melts and disappears. The cook yells, "Order up!" I try to think of something to say, but I fail.

Daniel works his thin fingers over the beanie again. "I . . ." he starts but stops.

"Go on now," I tell him.

Daniel looks at me, and whatever I have made my life about shudders under the weight of its lie.

"I'd thought about it before then. Before you, I mean." Daniel works his hands together in front of him, knitting and reknitting them. "It's all like a dream now, you see. It's like this dream that I'm trying to remember after all these years. I had wanted to be released. Not from you. Not like that. Just the . . ." Daniel puts a fist to his chest and looks at his daughter.

I look at them. Both of them are different now. Strangers to whatever versions of themselves they were together.

"I'd been waiting for my dad to go before I did it. I thought it'd hurt him too much, you know?"

Susan is crying one tear at a time. They run down her cheeks in single streams until she wipes them away with her sleeve.

"I needed to be done. I needed a release from the hopelessness. You see?"

Susan puts her hand on Daniel's. I watch her jerk away from the cold she wasn't expecting, but she recovers herself and grips his hand.

OUTSIDE THE DELI, we stand in the cold air. I take a picture of them together. Susan and Daniel. Clouds of her breath and only her breath floating upward. They each smoke a cigarette, the same brand. I think, at least they have this in common. Maybe this is what progress looks like. But then I remember: they already have death in common. You might wonder, a guy like me, whether I'm ready for it. That great big beyond that's rushing toward us. I worry less about that than about coming back, rising again years later and seeing this world all dressed up in a new wardrobe and smelling different. Like running into an old girlfriend you haven't seen in years, and you struggle to recognize her or the man you were when you were with her. I'll have to come back and have weekly meetings with a guy like me. Some working stiff leading my stiff body around the ashes of my past, trying to make amends for a life already ended. Maybe he'll have me go back and apologize to Deb if she's still kicking. I wouldn't mind that, I suppose. Maybe she'll be back, too, and we'll start all over again. Two dead divorcés with all the time in the world on our skeletal hands. Till death do us unite.

DANIEL AND I are driving back north to Seattle when I decide to take us to the ocean. It's still a hundred miles away, but as soon as we take the junction and head west, I can taste the saltwater in the air. I roll down the windows and let the breeze hit us. Daniel stares forward, his shoulders slumped. I wonder what Doug would do in this moment, but I think that maybe the ocean can do the thing that needs to be done.

Daniel never asks where we're going, but an hour and a half later, we drive down the hill and the ocean spreads out before us. I take us to the state park and we pull into a sandy spot. I get out and breathe in the air, and Daniel pulls himself out of the car and follows me down the sandy bluff.

We stay at the beach awhile, not talking, just picking up sand dollars and digging our toes in the cold, wet muck. Eventually we end up back at the car, watching the surf.

I ask Daniel, "You gonna go back and see her again?"

But he shakes his head. "I'm just a bad memory."

Then Daniel explains it to me. Why they want to sleep so much. He tells me to think about an afternoon. A warm one, with a slight cooling breeze coming in through an open window. Think about the moment, he says, right after you've just made love, and you're lying on that couch feeling the breeze. And you know you're falling asleep. There's a calm tingle to your whole body. Like you're feeling every single cell you've got. You know you're drifting off. That you'll wake up again in a bit. But right in that moment, that perfect moment, your eyelids drop like anvils, and each time you just barely manage to open them again. Fighting sleep just cause of the way it feels. The rest of your head and body are clear and weightless. Like you're floating. And then, and this is when Daniel places his cold hands over mine. And then, when you've struggled enough and you give in, the euphoria laps and washes over you like a warm wave and your last blink turns into sleep. You think, I'm going to sleep now, and then I'm going to wake up to this perfect moment.

He stops talking, and the sounds of the ocean wash over us. I want to say something to Daniel after this, when his eyes are searching mine and his grip is so strong. I want to give him the absolution that walking death has robbed him of. But I don't have that to offer. I won't tell a dead man about God's grace.

I can only write that Case 7 shows progress and drive us the long way home.

Drew McCutchen earned a BA in creative writing at the University of Washington. His fiction has appeared in the *Baltimore Review* and is forthcoming from *Pleiades Magazine*. Drew is an assistant editor at *Fifth*

Wednesday Journal. A Washington native, Drew enjoys backpacking in the Cascade and Olympic mountain ranges. He lives in Seattle with his partner, Brooke, and their cat, Henry. Without the support of his friends and family, his writing would not exist. He is currently at work on a novel.

EDITORS' NOTE

Our editorial process is a collective one. The day we discussed "Black Dog" by Alex Terrell, the most common reaction was awe. This story is wild and transformative—but it also unsettles. Terrell addresses the human body as a site for the animal element, a multiplicity of identities, as well as an inheritance of mythology and trauma. As readers, we felt like children, standing on the cusp of an ancient and terrifying forest, where past and parallel selves trail behind like ghosts and stalk like predators.

Cat Ingrid Leeches, editor
Jackson Saul, assistant editor
Black Warrior Review

BLACK DOG

Alex Terrell

SHE WOULD AWAKEN in the woods. In sunlight. Underneath trees and laying on rocks.

Roots.

Unsheathed and exposed to all manner of elements. But she was warm. Leaves were twisted and mashed into her hair, but she could not feel them on her scalp. This was a reminder that her hair was not hers. It belonged to the girls in India who cried when their heads were shaved and their sorrow could be bought and sold for $79.99 a pack at Lovely's on Bright Street. She'd only needed three packs.

She paid her cousin, Drea, sixty to put the weave in and another twenty for the pizza she ordered. That investment now had leaves attached to it. And mud, she found.

She also found that there were no tracks, from small animals or large ones. No drag marks. And no explanation for the scratches on her arms and ankles. The bottoms of her feet were stained black like she'd been dancing around in pitch. Her fingernails, which had been short last night, were now long.

She stood on unsteady legs, knees knocking together, quaking under the weight of her body. Out the corner of her eye, she saw several versions of herself dressed in all white, and as a buzzing behind her eyes settled into a slow ache, she thought, *How did they follow me here?*

THE NIGHT WRAPPED its great arms around her, hanging on her shoulders. The cool air, a haint riding her back. She remembered when she was little that she had asked Momma why she was painting Grandma Pearl's porch blue and Momma had said, "Haints can't cross water. The blue confuses them." So she avoided very blue water. As she'd watched Momma run the paintbrush over rows of chipped paint, she'd thought that she might be a ghost and how strange and wonderful it might be if she couldn't cross the porch. But she was able to plant her feet firmly on those dried blue planks. She was a real girl after all. Or maybe haints were just smarter than Momma thought. She didn't understand until she was older that being a real girl didn't mean you couldn't be invisible. Even now up on the roof, she was a ghoul.

She took in the scene of the rooftop bacchanalia, eyes drifting over sweating bodies and strung lights. The crowd was a mixed bag of hipsters, indie kids, pill-pushers, and weed dealers. It wasn't even midnight and almost everyone was wasted and writhing in agony against each other. Or maybe they just looked that way to her with their shirts clinging to their backs, hair greasy under knit caps, denim jackets dark blue from drinks being spilled on them all night. Io thought they looked miserable, but then she didn't like dancing. And she was sure she didn't like the city at all. She hated the way smoking a cigarette somehow tasted worse when the chemicals mingled with city air.

Io had realized early on that she had played the night to its full potential. She'd had a few shots of whiskey at the bar and bought a dime bag of weed off of Slim Jimmy. She's waited patiently for him to finish getting off with the pale-faced girl in the bathroom. He'd said, *Slide it under the door.* The transaction had taken place over thumping bass and underground in The Attic, where Io had had her first drink with Sola Delgado when they were sixteen-and-some-change. Sola had told Io to push her skirt up a bit before they went in—*Let them see your legs, Io*—and Io had waited outside of this same scratched up bathroom door while Sola lost her backdoor virginity to Slim Jimmy, who never discriminated based on age, he'd said. But that was when Io and Sola were Sola-and-Io. When they were fused at the hip like a chimera of bone and sinew and hair all one color. Sharing the same breath. Now, Io rarely saw Sola, except for the occasional glitch in the matrix when they were in the wrong place at the same time. Usually this was only for a few seconds before Io lost sight of Sola's bouncing curls pulled high into that infamous ponytail, another head in the crowd.

When Slim Jimmy had opened the door, the smell of sweaty body parts and hair had filled the space and this was about all the night could wring out, Io decided. He'd put the baggie in her hand, lingering there longer than she would have liked. His fingers, burnt from smoking joints to the bottom, passing over Io's palm slowly.

Thanks, Jimmy.

Up on the rooftop, Io watched phantoms of herself walking back and forth. She was standing by the couch wearing a leather skirt and tights, a shirt that showed her stomach and a silver ball that sparkled on her tongue when she talked. Io-Leather-Skirt laughed with her whole body at a joke someone said and the crowd consumed her.

Another one was standing near the makeshift coatrack, wearing jeans and a sweater that fell loose in all of the right places. This Io stood with better posture and her lipstick was a shade darker than Io-Leather-Skirt's lipstick. She talked easily with a couple of girls. Neither were prettier than the other. Neither were prettier than Io, but she could not see this. Io-Leather-Skirt watched through keyholes made by arms and legs as she was brought down further by the small crowd. Io-in-Jeans didn't notice Io-Leather-Skirt's demise, because she was admiring herself in the reflection in one of the girls' glasses. Io-in-Jeans was cornered by the white girls with talks of a trip to Panama City Beach, and eventually, she disappeared into the wall behind her. Io-in-Jeans's untimely departure was witnessed by Io-in-Red, standing near the drink area flirting with three guys.

Io watched those same specters fall off the rooftop, run into the door, and nearly crash into other people before she slipped back in her skin. She looked down at her shirt, the color of bland chicken, and her thighs, sheathed in leggings that were worn out from too many wears. Her hair was pulled back and she wore too much makeup, which covered patches of dark skin and craters from years of picking at her cheeks. And as she watched the night pass in front of her, she knew she had gone unnoticed yet again. That she had been little more than a wall fixture, sitting crooked and undisturbed. She knew the specters would have fared better than she, because she was barely there. And they were much more than ghosts.

She came back to herself. For Io, sometimes the walls of the world were fuzzy, and she found herself wading through a daydream. She took in the rooftop scene one last time before knocking back another shot. As vodka hit her tongue, her eyes were drawn over to the door. The man wore nice clothes. Autumn colors were a compliment to his deep brown skin. With full lips and a prominent nose, he was beautiful. Did he know he was? Did he notice how eyes drifted to him? How the rooftop drank him in?

She thought she smelled him. She thought then that she could almost taste him. Pheromones? Were those real? Did they apply to humans? Weren't humans also animals? Yes, she could almost taste him. But she couldn't place the flavor. Like *presque vu*, Momma would say. Having that thing on the tip of your tongue. Momma's tongue was a creole one. When Momma spoke, it conjured smoke and mossy cypress trees. Tupelo trees. Sentinels of the swamp. It conjured the bayous and *what did you say gal?* Io hadn't been to the bayou since she was small. She hadn't remembered the swamp except through peepholes in Momma's tongue. But she was cityside now. Long gone from those dirt roads. From plantation homes.

She thought still that she could smell him. Not really him, but what parts of him came through the air. She wondered if he could smell her from where he was. Could he almost taste her? Would he want to?

Usually the whiskey did the job, keeping that dark voice out. But sometimes, when the moon was full, she found herself in stranger tides. She found that dark voice poking holes in her mind, turning into a thousand tiny mouths that said, *He'll look you up and down and then pass you up for one of these white girls.*

But the man was still alone and she watched him. The way he moved took up space. And not just for the sake of occupying space, but because his body—which looked both powerful and full of grace—required it. He didn't look at her. He also seemed not to notice how she stalked him with her eyes low or how every girl up on the roof tracked him.

And then his eyes settled on her, which unsettled her. She'd been made. She buttoned her coat and wrapped her scarf about her neck tighter and headed for the door.

"I'm Jude," he said as she passed him.

She almost turned to see who he was talking to.

"This is the part where you tell me yours," he said. She could hear his smile as he spoke.

"Io," she said with her back to him.

"Eye-oh." He said her name slowly. "Unusual name."

"No stranger than Jude," she said. "It short for Judas?"

"Nah, just Jude," he said. He broke away from the party. "This party is kinda . . . well, it ain't shit."

"Hasn't been for a few hours," she said, still with her back to him. She kept her jacket closed tight, because she'd become aware of her body then. The burden of being noticed.

She didn't hear him move, just felt him moving closer. His body heat emanated toward her, sliding through the kinks in her chill like a hot comb. Who notices ghouls?

"You wanna go somewhere?" he asked. "To talk, I mean."

She turned to him then and said, "Uh, no."

He stepped closer to her. "Can I at least give you my number?"

"What for?" she asked.

"So we can talk."

"Ghosts don't talk. They only moan," she said.

He looked at her like she'd knocked some of his wind out. "And I was worried about being forward . . ."

They didn't say anything for a moment.

"You're weird," he said, and now their bodies seemed to be leaning into each other like planets falling into the same inscrutable orbit. Momma had always said you'd know when a man wanted you.

"I have to go," she said.

"Graveyard calling?" he asked.

"Something like that," she said, turning away. She passed the fallen specters on the way out. They stood in a group, hands on their hips, heads shaking. Their bodies still bore the traits of their deaths. One of them said, "What's *wrong* with you?"

IO SETTLED IN on a bench and watched buses pass, not catching any of them. She hadn't even looked to see where they were going. She thought of Slim Jimmy and a little about Sola, but mostly about the many ways in which a night with Jude *could have* gone. It wasn't long before the other Ios showed themselves and took turns hitting her on the back and saying, very close to her ears, "He was out of your league anyway." Sometimes their cries became so loud that she was sure others would hear. She decided to forget the night by counting passersby, but as Jude came into her line of sight, she realized he was still in her crosshairs. She put her hood up to hide herself as he passed, only to get up and follow his tracks to Johanna's Coffeehouse. She stood on the other side of the glass, because she felt safer there.

Was the glass there for his protection or for hers?

It turned out that Jude wasn't a coffee man. He preferred tea, with lots of sugar. Io watched as a blond-haired girl tore several packets and mixed them in behind the counter. The girl leaned into him, tossing her hair over her shoulder. She bared her chest for him. She had the most saccharine sweet smile that Io had ever seen. Io was sure that smile was sweet enough to sugar Jude's tea by itself.

Jude sat in the corner alone and Io watched him flip through a book that had been resting on the bookshelf beside him. She imagined him inviting her in. She imagined what they'd talk about.

"I like sweetness. It's my kryptonite," he'd say.

Io took her tea without sugar and her coffee black. "My mom said sugar is of the devil."

"Where's your mom from?"

"Below the Mason-Dixon line."

He'd laugh then. The kind of laugh that caught in your chest and clawed at your insides, splitting them. Io supposed she hated those kinds of laughs. Those kinds of interactions too. Perhaps any real interaction.

"You look . . . pensive," he'd say after a few sips.

"I am," she'd say. "I'm just thinking."

He'd lean into her in a way that muted all of the noise around them and knit them up tight. "What are you thinking?"

"I dunno."

"Not about forever, I mean. Just right now," he'd say.

She'd shrug. "Honestly?"

He'd nod.

"I'm thinking of why I came here with you. I don't know you. I'm not sure if I like you," she'd say.

"Fair enough," he'd say, taking another sip.

"But even more so, I'm thinking about our relationship. And I don't mean we're in a relationship. I mean how we are in relation to each other."

"Go on."

"Like how every time you meet someone, even if you just bump into them on the subway or accidentally knock into them on the street, it's a relationship. It's like they've seen you and you've seen them. Probably for the first time in your life, even though you've been stomping around in the same spaces probably for a while now. Or maybe not at all. Or maybe they just got to town and you had the audacity to run into them. To leave your impression on them. And for them to leave their impression on you. Like, who do you think you are, right? Who do we think we are?" She'd take a sip of her coffee and come back to herself. "I usually don't talk that much. Sorry."

He'd lean back in his chair and stretch a little. "I've been told that I have that effect on people. They just bear their souls to me. I like to listen."

"It shows," she'd say. His eyes were almond shaped. She'd let herself admire them then, but only a little.

"I was just gonna head home in a few," he'd say then. "You're welcome to come. No expectations."

"No expectations?" She'd wonder if that then was the time to tell him she'd never slept with anyone. She'd decide against it.

"None."

"Momma told me not to go home with strange men. She said strange men turn into strange animals."

"Momma might be right," he'd say.

From there, Io would walk home with him and he would show her his skin. She'd see that it was made from flesh that smelled like warm spices and that it tasted like cayenne pepper. Io would find this out. Jude would find out that Io held honeycombs. That she was a stinging thing. That she was prickly and also soft. That her skin was electric. And how they arrived at this moment when they both realized they wanted each other would be a convergence of limbs and soft strokes. Teeth and hair and scratches. Warmth and wetness and the rush of blood. She'd climb the walls of him and he'd welcome her mouth with tempered muscle and veins. Together they'd make a chimera, even if only fused at their spines and where their hips met. It would be then that Io would wish for that cold night air and its chill to find them under the mountain of blankets on Jude's bed. She imagined that his loft was artfully decorated, but she'd only see his pillow.

IO WALKED, FEET beating hard against pavement. She passed houses, banal driveways, sprinklers that were still on. Midnight showers. She stopped short and stood under a canopy of trees on her left. She saw the moon pierce through clouds and smog and bathe the woods in white. It must have been there, covered in moonlight, that she first sensed it. It was a barely-there sensation that made her ears perk up, like a dog whistle singing that which only she could hear. She couldn't make it out among the trees. Partially hidden by branches and the rest of it by shadow. Or perhaps the rest of it wasn't there. And maybe it never was.

She felt it walking close, and sometimes far away. Fast, and sometimes slow. On all fours and on two feet. On all fours again. Eyes to the ground. She listened for its feet and for its breath. For its pause and its start. It tracked her, never moving in front of her. But in the periphery it rested. An intangible shadow thing lurking, prowling. Its body seemed strong. She imagined visible breath from the cold night puffing through its nostrils. A long, forked tongue. It followed at a hundred yards away. It kept its distance and she did not look at it. She did not hear it stop. And though she wanted to, she did not relieve that tension in her neck to turn to it. Where were the Ios now? Had they been run off by the lurking thing?

It felt familiar, she realized. Like something she had known. Like something that she almost knew. Or had perhaps once known. That Which Followed stalked her home.

She let herself in the house, keys knocking against her wrist as her hand shook. As That Which Followed waited and did not draw closer. She did not look for it under moonlight. She did not look for it when she was on the safe side of the door or when she closed her window before bed. She left it waiting for her, down below.

THAT NIGHT SHE dreamed of a dark body covering her own. Of strong legs prying hers open. Of her welcoming it. Of sharp teeth dragging across her skin. Of warm breath. Of cold wind. She dreamed of the blue porch.

WHEN SHE AWOKE in the woods, in sunlight, underneath trees and laying on rocks, an ache had set up shop in between her thighs. There was a buzzing there. Honeycombs. Like a hive lived there. Like she'd been colonized.

SHE RINSED THE dirt off first and then touched herself in the shower until she felt her breath hitch in her throat. She finished, but the buzzing soon returned with a pointy reckoning that almost stung. She clenched. She squeezed.

She was strategic when taking out her weave, which was ruined by the mud. She clipped out the pieces of thread that held the weave together and let the whole thing unravel in the sink. What was left were the coarse curls of her hair, and tender scalp. She kept the nails long.

•

She had a hole in her stomach when next she woke. It needed filling. For breakfast, she ate eggs and a piece of steak from the fridge, raw. She ran it under the sink in hot water to get the ice off. She thawed it and spiced it.

Momma came down at quarter after seven wearing her bathrobe and her head scarf. She wore full makeup—*Io, I can't leave the house without my face on*—and big pearl earrings. She kissed Io on the cheek. "Didn't hear you come in last night."

Io scooted forward on her stool and crossed her legs one way and then the other. "I got in late."

Momma slid the coffee filter in and closed the top with a snap. "You be careful because the news said there were some robberies a couple of nights ago and some man was talkin' about how he saw a coyote or somethin' like it in the woods."

"We don't get coyotes," Io said. A lightning strike snapped through her, making her shiver below the waist. She throbbed.

"I know," Momma said. "Where's mine?"

"Eggs are on the stove," Io said, uncrossing her legs and then crossing them again.

Momma busied herself with the business of making toast and putting her cold eggs in the microwave. She poured herself a big cup of coffee and sat down beside Io.

"Since when do you eat your meat rare?" Momma asked. "It'll make you sick."

Her walls thrummed against each other. Buzzing. Rippling. "I like it like this."

"Since when?"

Buzz. "Trying something new, Momma. That all right?" The meat slid through her teeth easily, blood filling up the cavity of her mouth with each piece. But she wished it was warm. And that it was fresh.

Momma tore into her toast. "I guess, but don't come cryin' to me when you get sick."

"I'm already sick," Io said.

EACH TIME SHE woke up in the woods, it was after she'd dreamed about a black dog standing over her. This reminded her of a story Momma told her on her sixteenth birthday about the Rougarou. Momma told her that when Grandma Pearl told it to her, she'd called it the Swamp Wolf of Nawlins. Grandma Pearl told Momma that the Rougarou wasn't a what but a who. Grandma Pearl told this story to Momma on the porch right before Momma left for prom. Grandma Pearl pulled Momma close and said. "In 'dem trees, it waits. Watchin'. It's hungry. In the swamp. Dat thing.

"It can smell a man on ya," Grandma Pearl told Momma. She said that when it caught the scent of a girl who was now a woman, it saw her blood. Grandma Pearl didn't know that the only thing that watched Momma was Momma's cousin, Perry. Or that Momma had lost her virginity in the backseat of Aunt Rena's car. Perry: age twenty. Momma: age twelve. Details: unclear. Momma had left the part about Perry out. She'd just laughed to Io and said, "Just an old story."

IN CLASS, THE buzzing moved from between her legs into her head and her chest. She felt the prickling of small hairs protruding from places where it had no business being. Her bones moved under her skin, popping, muted, a mortar and pestle grinding in her sockets. She rolled her shoulders. They rolled back.

And on her walk home, she felt That Which Followed, following closely. Perhaps it never left, but just retreated when the sun chased the shadows off. Under moonlight it was relentless and it stalked her at close range, but she did not look at it. She didn't know much about it, but what she did know of it was that it was the same height as her.

Io SAT IN a bath, because that seemed to ease the buzzing in her stomach. She searched *buzzing, head, stomach, legs, vagina* on her phone. It returned no results.

THE BUZZING FELT sort of like bites. Like a thousand tiny mouths hummed on her skin and had colonized her head and chest. Had spread between her thighs, and to her hair, her nails, and her ears. It was also accompanied by an itch in the deep tissue of her skin. This was soothed, slightly, by laying on the bathroom floor and excessive masturbation. This did next to nothing except increase her affinity for bloody, sinewy, raw meats. She picked up a pound of steak and chicken livers from the grocery. She ate them out of a brown paper bag while Momma was at work.

Io SAT IN a bath, chest buzzing, and searched *black dog* on her phone. It returned several results.

•

SHE AWOKE IN a cold sweat. She turned on her fan and went downstairs for water. She wandered down, holding tight to the bannister, searching for the last step. Momma was sleeping on the couch when she passed, but she saw something cast in shadow roving near.

That Which Followed stood over Momma on two legs with claws long and sharp perched just above her torso, back hunched, hair sprawling from its body. A mane of black hair. Its teeth dripped saliva onto Momma's head.

"Stop," Io said. "Leave her out of it."

That Which Followed didn't move. It kept its stance, but pointed to the door. A few seconds later, the door crept open soundlessly.

"Okay," Io said.

Io wandered past the park and down Bright Street to the wood's edge, trailing That Which Followed at twenty paces. That Which Followed walked into a clearing of trees on two hind legs. Once she passed through that invisible mouth, that threshold, the buzzing ceased. She imagined that the woods were the swamp, that these were one and the same. Wasn't a swamp just the woods drowning? But this swamp's water was clear blue instead of the murky green it should have been. Bluer-than-the-porch water. She backed away from it.

"It isn't supposed to look like that," she said to That Which Followed. To the Ios: "Why is it so blue?"

That Which Followed circled her then, nipping at her ankles and snarling. It urged her in.

The Ios raised their voices and Io thought how wonderful it might be to see them die. She unzipped her dress and stepped out of it, and let it sink underwater. She waded farther in, and could see her wavy reflection in the water. She looked so unlike them. And the water felt nicer than she thought it would, and warmer. She could hear cicadas in the trees. She could feel the swamp water touching her ankles and then her knees. On the bank of her imagined swamp sat her phantom selves dressed in white. Sacrificial white. Sacrificial rites. One held a knife. One held a spear. Their faces were half naked and half tribal paint. They wore many rings.

"The water is so nice," she said to the Ios. She knew they could not stand for her to enjoy something without them enjoying it more. "Come in."

Io invited them in one at a time. The swamp changed to green as they entered, and stained their white clothes. She pushed their heads underneath the water. She held them there for many beats. Beat. Beat. Beat. Io-in-Red succumbed. She's dead. And when one was done, she invited in the next. Io-Leather-Skirt. She struggled more than her sisters. But the flailing ceased. Io could feel each death in her own body and in her own breath. She felt the pain and then the release.

That Which Followed met her at the swamp's edge and allowed her to take its hand. She realized that the hand she held was first a claw and then her own soft hand. And then nothing. She saw Jude sitting there on the bank, watching. She felt the bones in her arms elongating and her skin spreading to meet the new demands of this new body. She let her neck crack and split. She let her feet lift off of the ground and rest on her haunches. She let the black hair crawl to her fingers and then her toes.

This body was wondrous. It was trees and dry ground. It was

sold rock and steel. She let a feral cry escape her lips and let the water capsize her.

When she came up for air, which was quite some time later, because she liked the swamp floor, Jude sat there still.

"Yes," she said. "I'd like to go somewhere with you."

Alex Terrell is currently pursuing an MFA. Her research interests include representations of individuated Black experience and Black bodies, magical realism, Afrofuturism, and how women speak in silent spaces. Alex resides in the Northeast, but she is a Tennessee girl.

EDITOR'S NOTE

What appealed to me on my first reading of "New Years in La Calera" by Cristina Fríes was the compelling sense of place in the story, a place that turns out to be both real and surreal nearly from the opening, when the narrator conflates the actual landscape of the Andes with the "dips and peaks" of her grandmother's body. Like some writers from the American South, Cristina Fríes seems to see place in fiction as a dramatic force for narrative, and to my reading, this is what propels her story—this and some beautiful writing and some extraordinarily well-imagined scenes.

When we came to discuss "New Years in La Calera" in an editorial meeting, I was surprised that the first editor to speak also began by talking about the importance of place in the story. Our discussion took off from that point, and, in uncharacteristic fashion, we elected to accept the story for *Epoch* after just one meeting.

Michael Koch, editor
Epoch

NEW YEARS IN LA CALERA

Cristina Fríes

NEW YEARS, WE believe, was four days ago, but the party down the hill has not stopped since then. Those who walk through our hills—the drug traffickers, the guerrilla, the runaways—pause to listen to the boleros echoing against the valley walls, and know this place must be some kind of refuge. Without owning calendars but instead sensing the time of year through their memories or by watching the movement of the stars, they can tell it's close to the first day of the new year. From the big house down the hill, the drum rhythms beat their way through the tall stalks of the tree ferns, inviting them to celebrate. I can even hear the party from our home when I've been bad and have to spend the night in the basement with the butterflies, blowing them off my nose with my sleeping, slow breath.

While some people who pass by our home will be dressed in muddy jeans, holding the hands of children who wear the faded clothes of their older siblings, others will be in green army suits with their pants tucked loosely into their boots. This migration, I've learned, is evidence of the warfare occurring in the rest of the country. Here, on the hill where we have always lived, we are not involved. I watch the people pass by us like streams while we stay put, stubborn as rocks. My grandparents have lived in this house since they became the groundskeepers, so many years ago they can't remember when they first arrived, unsure if it was when they were children or married adults, if the dogs were theirs or if they belonged to the farm, if there was war or peace. From the doorway, we can see the big house through the fog. The house is taller than all of the trees, and looks as though it has always been there, firmly built into the landscape that has not changed since prehistoric times, dense with enormous tree ferns and colorful flowers the size of my head. Sometimes when I'm not doing my chores and I hike through these hills in search of mushrooms and grasshoppers, I imagine traveling onward, past these hills and over beyond the precipice that drops thousands of meters to banana farms and warmer weather, never stopping in one place but instead moving on across the country like the groups of people I so often see passing through my home.

The Andes burst up around us at all angles, like the dips and peaks of my grandmother's body, her wide breasts when she lies in her bed, fat filling up every inch of the mattress, her belly rising above her sleeping, weeping face. There were times when I thought, from beneath the floorboards where I could hear her as I do now, that she was crying because of something I'd done. Over time, though, I've come to realize that it's beyond my control—there is something haunting about a time that is lost to her, and that has caused her to deteriorate. I hear her cry about her ailments, though I know she can't possibly be ill—she is much too stubborn. It's cancer! she yells from above the basement, It's a tumor in my heart, filling me up every day. I'm like a cow's tit.

From down here, I hear the night nurse scurry around our house, her miniature feet scuffling across what sounds like the kitchen tiles, fetching my grandmother her tea, her rosaries, the things with which she plans to get cured. Someday I'm going to burst, and you're all going to get hit right in the face, she says while praying to the Virgin Mary. You're all going to drown in my tumor. Then she quiets down and falls asleep in the middle of a sentence, in the middle of her meal, giving the night nurse a sense of relief as soon as the bedroom goes silent.

The hatch to the basement is flush with the wooden floorboards, and if I kick it hard enough from down here, its vibrations must make our basement look like it's haunted with angry ghosts. Looking up through a crack in the floor, I see the night nurse's skirt glide overhead in the direction of the living room. While my grandmother rests, the night nurse spends her afternoons sitting on the couch and watching the dogs from the window—how many we have now, I couldn't say, because every day some of them die and some new ones are born and there is no point in counting or naming them. I can hear the night nurse speak above me, but I can barely understand what she is saying—her voice is like the flapping of wings, so agitated and airy that it fills up every space in the house, a white humming, a mosquito in the ear. I yell at her from below the floorboards to go milk the cow, feed the dogs, just to make it stop. I've had enough with the butterflies as it is. If my grandfather were here, he'd be the one to tell her to begin preparing breakfast, made with whatever ingredients he's stolen from the pastures, but since he spends his days tending to them—the carrot and potato fields, the fat cows and surly goats—that duty falls on me.

My grandfather only comes home for dinner, and just before dawn he disappears into the hills again. Every morning when I get up to begin my chores, I see a trail of his footprints leading away from our home, down the tiny scoop of our hill, beyond our cow's stable, and then I can't see them anymore. His footprints cover the hills of our valley, but I am never eager to follow them.

Last night I slept in the basement, and since there is no sunlight, the footsteps and the night nurse's voice through the floorboards are my only clues that my punishment is finally over. I hear her unlock the hatch, and I rush to climb out.

In the living room, I shake off like a wet dog the butterflies that have latched onto my hair and knees. I stretch out my joints and bend my neck before pulling on my apron, which was once my grandmother's. It is still too large around the breasts and waist, as I have yet to fill out, but I'm confident it won't be long until I do. I stand in front of the reflective surface of a golf trophy my grandfather stole from the big house and in it I see my own curvature, or what I hope will be soon.

In my reverie, I almost don't hear the knock at the door. It must be the escaped hostages who walk through our valley—who else would knock so quietly, with so much shame? The night nurse, nervous whenever we have visitors, hides in the kitchen while I greet the group of men at our doorstep.

Wearing jeans splattered with dried mud, they look around the house with modesty, asking if we have any water or milk to spare, calling me *su merced*, as if I were some kind of high-class city girl. Why yes, we have plenty, I tell them, even though we don't—our old cow is as moody and as close to death as my grandmother. But it's polite to offer your guests as much as you can provide. We are a pit stop in the middle of their long journeys across the country, and they will be grateful for anything they can get.

Our house lies outside of the big city, but we are hidden in the mountains, covered by their swooping shadows. The escaped hostages and the guerrilla soldiers who once kidnapped them camp and carry out their work in places like this, hiding in the jungle, and traveling by foot across our country's densest and most secret terrains. Whether they're soldiers or prisoners, I am sure that when these people hide in the fog that rolls in from the north, covering everything but the tips of tree ferns and pointed mountain bluffs, they must sometimes look around and think, *Qué belleza.*

It is a beautiful place, no? I ask these men, because despite their harrowed looks, I can see that they must be in awe of their surroundings. I watch them as they sip our herbal tea—some that I assume my grandfather has stolen from the big house down the hill. I tell the night nurse to bring us some pan de yuca, and she scuttles in her slippers into the kitchen, whispering things none of us can hear, while my grandmother screams at us from her room, saying, I am barely alive! I am tethered to life by a leg hair!

I ask them where they've been, how they've managed to trek through the steep mountainsides, and where they plan to go next. They don't answer my questions, too polite to reveal anything specific, instead responding with platitudes and smiles and bowed heads to show their respect. It's mostly light chatter with the escaped hostages, whenever groups of them come knocking. They are afraid of saying too much to a girl about what they've seen, or they're shy. So I resign myself to watching them drink their tea in silence, wipe their moustaches with their ragged sleeves, and then march down our hill, toward the main house on the plot of land. The drumming sounds from the landkeeper's house carry through the valley, reverberate through the trees, and reach our house as a quiet beat, as quiet but as incessant as the night nurse's voice. While doing housework, I'll sometimes find my hips swaying to its almost imperceptible rhythm. I wish the men a Happy New Year and, watching them march on, I can tell that today the hostages will make another stop on their journey to celebrate with the man who owns this land and who, like all of us, is unsure of the exact day of the year.

While my grandmother lies in bed, the night nurse tends to her health, and my grandfather disappears in the landscape of our valley, I perform the household duties. Today, I have to scrub the muddy footprints off the floor that my grandfather left after returning from his campesino work. Despite rarely being home, he leaves traces. With the crumbs of his dinner bread, I can see that he paces in the living room, which is small and full of patched-up furniture, and today, I spot new stolen objects scattered around the house: a lace tablecloth over the dinner table, and an empty vase on the windowsill that is surely over one hundred years old. It looks so delicate and fine, like a bird's egg or a dandelion in the wind, that I am tempted to break it.

I have seen my grandfather fix fences that have been trampled, inject medications into the cows that, soon after, scatter madly across the landscape. I have seen him with his entire arm up the backside of a pregnant horse, and heard him break the neck of the smaller of the twins lying inside. I have also seen him kick the dogs, and I've seen his small, hunched figure hide around the back of the landowner's house before returning with stolen items bulging in his muddy overcoat. My grandmother, in response to his thievery, says, Watch out, or the Devil will tug on your penis in your sleep! When my grandfather removes his new belongings from his clothes, he says that the rich man owns so many nice things that he will never miss them. He says the rich man will blame guerrilla soldiers or escaped hostages, who are known for their robberies. I imagine the men who were just here stuffing their muddy sweaters with pots and pans, soccer balls and candelabras. Where would they put them? I wonder. Do they set up their new china on fallen logs and eat great feasts in the middle of the jungle?

After cleaning the floors, I do the work that the night nurse, who is frail of heart, refuses to do. Today, it's cleaning between my grandmother's flaps of fat. It takes what feels like hours, going through every crevasse with my sponge. Barely noticing my touch, she stays asleep—a loud, snoring boulder. When I wash my grandmother, I often fear she'll roll on top of me and trap me beneath her weight forever, and I'll never get my own chance to feast in the jungles.

By the time I finish, the sun has gone down, the dogs have curled into a ball of worms to keep warm through the night, and I'm covered in grime and dust. I go to the bathroom and take off my clothes and fill the tub with warm water. My grandmother used special soap in her baths when she was still slim enough to fit inside the tub. I pour in half the bottle and relish in its pinkish hues, its luxurious smell filling the bathroom with the scent of angels.

As I step into the soapy water, I hear my grandfather open the front door. He tells the night nurse to heat up some rice and beans. And now, I know, he is approaching the bathroom to wash his hands. I take a big gulp of air and then my face is wet and my head and all of me is underwater and it is quiet. Finally, I think, savoring the solitude. I can see nothing but the black behind my closed eyelids, feel nothing but the silence like electricity in my ears. I wonder, Is this how the hostages felt when bags were tied over their faces, when they were knocked over the head and made to feel nothing, the way my grandfather told me it happens when people are taken into the jungle? If it had been anything like being thrust underwater, I think, it must have felt, momentarily, like freedom.

And then, I feel my grandfather pulling chunks of my black, sudsy hair, and the cold air again on my face. What are you doing? he yells. What do you think we are, royalty?

It's true; I am taking a bubble bath. But after everything he has stolen, I don't see the problem with my indulgence. His jacket is bulging with half a dozen heavy objects, making him look fat and demented with his nostrils flaring like a boar's. His yelling wakes up my grandmother, who then begins screaming that nobody treated her like a queen in her whole life, that she never once got to use silver utensils or sleep on fur coats, that princesses don't exist, that in her day she would have done something I was unable to hear because by then I was already being shoved into the basement, and all I could hear was the awful beating of butterfly wings.

The basement has no windows. My grandfather's only attempt at making it livable was to throw in a cot with a blanket the size of a pillowcase around the time that I began making him angry because I'd been breaking his stolen objects. But even before he began his stealing, my grandfather would come home to broken dishes and ruined furniture. He'd look around at the mess and point his wrinkled finger at me and call me his *nieta de mierda*. I used to spill almost every drink or bowl of soup, but always by accident. It was the dogs, I'd tell him when he'd find a cracked mug or fallen flowerpot. Then train those damn dogs, he'd say. Put tags on them and put them to work. But when I'd see the dogs outside the kitchen window I couldn't help it. I'd run out and chase them through the pastures. They were much too beautiful just to watch—they seemed to dance on the tips of the blades of grass, with light paws and open mouths, as though singing.

And sometimes it really was the dogs who broke things. When I'd forget to close the front door, they'd run through the house in their messy, hypnotic way. They'd stumble through the living room, slipping on the tile with their claws loud like a woman's high heels. Past the kitchen, they'd burst through the door left ajar into my grandmother's room and crawl over her boulder of a body, and she'd curse them and call them the spawn of the devil, and then they'd continue on through the house, which is small so it wouldn't take long for them to tip over vases, drool on the countertops, discover food in places we would have never known food had been left. And then they'd be gone, their tails wagging high in the air so far away, almost out of sight, a cluster of brown and black moving steadily across the green, and around me all would be in ruins.

After seeing the house littered like this day after day, my grandfather finally said, Ha, now you will pay; now you will know how I feel about the mess you make in this house! He captured the butterflies from the pastures in glass jars and released them into our basement. Once the basement was full and we could hear the flapping of wings from outside, he shoved me in and locked the hatch. I see you running through the fields with your head in the clouds like the damn butterflies, he said. They're omens, butterflies; they bring about disorder. So now you will learn what it's like to live in chaos! he yelled, while my grandmother screamed something else, something I couldn't hear.

He started punishing me like this three years ago or the year before that. I can't be sure—I, too, have trouble keeping track of time. It's even harder when I'm in the basement. I've grown into the habit of counting my thoughts before they drift somewhere else, hiding in a new territory of my mind, as a way to determine how much time has passed. Every time I come here the cot is somewhere different. Now, naked and wet from the bubble bath, I cannot find it, although the basement is small and there aren't very many places it could have hidden. There are no lights, so my senses are reduced to touch, smell, hearing, taste, and intuition, which is the only sense women have that men don't, I once heard my grandmother say before she got so huge she couldn't get out of bed. We can see the things that are just marginally visible, like ghosts or the emotions of men. But now I cannot intuit where the cot is in this basement, and the butterflies seem to have multiplied, making it harder to sense with my other senses where I am and what I should do. I try and I try, but I can't count my thoughts yet. Sitting down on the cold floor, naked and soaking wet, I hold my knees until I am perfectly still. Shhhhhh, I tell myself, stop screaming.

IN THE MORNING, the night nurse opens the hatch and a little ray of sunlight pours into the basement. Come, she breathes, hurry before they all fly out. And I do. My grandmother sees me crawl out, covered in butterflies—purple, orange, green spots on my naked body—and yells that I look like the plague. Stay out of my room; you'll kill me with your breath! You'll bring this country to ruin!

Sometimes I feel sorry for my grandmother, listening to her grotesque rants. She used to tell me about the days when her waist was smaller than her hips and men would take her to dance salsa at the bars in the city where she was born, and about the times when cities were made up of houses rather than apartment buildings and she could roam through both city and countryside without fear of strange men kidnapping her. And she spoke of the time she felt her past and present intermingle and she became confused with the timeline of her life. She found it hard to tell the difference between what was old and new, ugly and beautiful, whether the men on the street were flirting with or threatening her, which was why she came to this valley where the confusion of the city could never reach her. This valley is a place where time becomes stagnant, she said, and it weighed down on her until her body grew to be as round as a guava and her body sagged like sandbags and she never stood up straight again. Now, from her bedroom, she screams, Girls! Butterflies! Clean up my fat!, her words becoming more insufferable and incomprehensible as time goes by.

As I prepare to begin my chores for the day, I notice that my grandfather has placed new objects around the house again. Expensive-looking silverware and a golden candelabra decorate the dinner table now. The landkeeper's framed family portraits have been placed on our walls, as though they were those of our ancestors. The new decorations make us look like we're cultured and have good taste in art. It feels, somehow, like a special occasion. I don't want to break any of it. Looking around, I think, Maybe this year will be a year of decadence. I imagine the house filled with men and women in fancy clothes. I listen for the sound of women's heels against the tile. And even my grandmother might participate—we could cover her in lace and serve tea and cookies on her broad belly, if she behaves.

I'd hate to soil my nicest dress with the grime from my chores, but I wear it anyway, for the new year. There's a butterfly latched onto my sleeve and I slap it off in a hurry. How awful, I think, these winged vermin.

Through the window I notice some men in green army suits hiking up the hill toward our house. They carry guns, and ammunition dangles around their necks like jewels, glistening in the morning light. They are radiant. I wait by the window, trying to hide behind the curtains so that they don't think I'm too eager. The night nurse scurries from my grandmother's room to the kitchen, pretending to be too preoccupied with my grandmother to tend to the guerrilla soldiers, who we both know will knock on our door. We are the only home for miles in every direction. The soldiers have the dark look of the indigenous Chibchas, but as they work their way up the hill they tear through the tall grasses like colonists, growing larger in the landscape from speck to toy soldier as they approach the house, until they are so huge they fill the entire window frame, so close that now they knock on the glass in front of my nose, looking me straight in the eye.

Buenos días, I say, opening the door. They nod their heads. I can't help but wish I were wearing something more mature. I look at their rifles and I want to hold one, but I'm too embarrassed to ask. They look heavy, and my bony arms would probably break just by touching them.

Can I offer you anything? I ask the guerrilla soldiers.

They are men who know what they want—without hesitating, they say, Give us some coffee.

In our living room, the guerrilla soldiers sit on my grandfather's ruined couch, while dogs run in and out of the house as they please. I bring out a steaming pot, and pour fresh coffee into the china that my grandfather stole, which I have not yet had the heart to break. The floral patterns are much too beautiful.

I pour myself some coffee too, although I hate the taste. Once everyone is still, I notice they are sparkling. Their ammunition is made of what looks like the shiniest of gold. They sit before me like princes, and instead of asking them about their travels as I had planned, I just stare at them, as though they're statues at the Gold Museum in the city, which I've never had the chance to visit and which I've only heard of through those who pass by our home. They say it holds the last of the gold of the indigenous people that was not stolen by conquistadores. They say it with pained voices, sorrowful, like it just happened yesterday, as though they can't tell the difference between a day and five hundred years.

Bueno, I say, tell me, what brings you to our valley? Have you been traveling for long? Sitting there, even in the yellow light of my grandfather's favorite lamp, they look like our dogs, with rounded muscles and angular jaws, perfect and fierce, but trained. They smile, putting their muddy boots on the coffee table between us. One of them lights himself a cigarette, puffing smoke into our living room. The soldiers look like they feel at home, and I'm relieved.

The one with the thick eyebrows says, Pues, niña, we've been traveling for weeks. We've seen more than you'd ever dream.

Like what? I'd like to ask. But I don't—the men are smiling in a secret sort of way, their mouths like closed locks, mocking. Instead I stand up and pour them more coffee, forcing my expression into one of mild interest rather than blazing curiosity. I fill each cup to the brim again, my hand never shaking. They'd never know how clumsy I can be. How proud my grandfather would be, how confused.

Niña, why do you not hesitate to serve us? the one with the thick eyebrows says, squeezing his cigarette between his fingers so tightly it looks as if the burning tobacco might fall to the carpet.

Well, I say, a bit of company never hurts. Most of the time I converse with the dogs, who really aren't such a nuisance if you adjust your lifestyle to match theirs. Run with them in the fields, drink water on all fours. All you have to do is adapt! I say gleefully, and then you see the world as they do. One of the dogs is licking the hand of the man with the moustache, drooling on his knee, and he slaps him away. I can feel myself blushing and, hoping I sound polite, I say, Now, would you like to tell me about your travels?

The man with the eyebrows smiles, staring at me. My grandfather often looks at me this way after hard days in the fields, and then in an instant, without saying a word, he'll throw me into the basement, even if I haven't done anything wrong. But these men are different. They are shining in gold.

Well, niña, there's not much to say, the man with the eyebrows says, blowing smoke. We see mountains, sleep in jungles, meet many, many people. But no women quite like you.

A woman! Even in this old dress. Beaming, I thank him, and say, I probably can't compete with the women at the party down the hill. They must be, I imagine, more graceful and beautiful than a campesina like me. Then I tell them about the man who hosts parties that last all day and night. His party must still be going on this morning. Do you hear that? I ask. That's the sound of cumbia and boleros.

Looking at them lined up on our small couch I realize how rude I've been because, isn't it obvious? They're hungry. Bring us some cookies, I yell out to the night nurse, who is hiding in the kitchen.

I see the men looking with interest at the stolen objects that decorate our living room and weigh down the thin walls that I've scrubbed clean so many times to please my grandmother. I know the appearance of order is important to her even if she cannot see it from her bedroom—but if she could see the house now, she'd feel like the high-class woman she never was. And now, here are the guerrilla soldiers, those who have seen faraway lands, sitting before me like princes. They are scanning the room, looking at the walls and the night nurse with eyes that seem incapable of sight, glazed over with a fog of sudden desire. Maybe they're impressed with our luxury—who would have thought our humble home held such marvels?

The night nurse brings a plate of our nicest chocolate cookies, which trembles in her hands. I smile, thinking how nicely the space of the house has filled today: the sounds of visitors, the thickness of it, the smell of leather boots and tobacco, the scraping of their fingernails against the couch, almost drowning out the sound of my grandmother who, from behind her bedroom door, yells, Who's out there? Imbeciles!

The dogs are licking up the crumbs on the floor, frantic with their hot breath, sniffing for more. Tell me, niña, one of the soldiers says. Come close, and tell me—he swings his arm out, gesturing toward the rest of the house, the luxurious ornaments—where is it that you got all of this?

For the first time, I feel like hugging my grandfather, wherever he might be. Well, I say, it all belongs to us—my family, I mean. The men look at me with faces whose meaning I cannot intuit, so I keep talking. The man just down the hill owns beautiful things like these, but more of them. And probably grander, I add to seem modest. Really, you must go visit his home. His party is still going on, can't you hear? They look out the window at the house with curiosity. These men make me want to tell them everything about our lives in this valley, but first I must apologize for the butterflies that have landed on the lapels of three of them. I bend toward the soldiers over the coffee table, swatting the insects away. I can see their nostrils flaring, feel their deep inhalations upon my hands. I explain how the butterflies have made themselves at home against my will. Don't worry, I despise them too! I say, and I suppose they think that I'm tougher than my fancy dress suggested to them upon first glance. A girl who hates butterflies. A girl who drinks from china teacups. Of course I am no ordinary campesina.

I pour another round. In the back of my mind where my intuition lives, I can hear my grandfather scolding me for being so tactless around strange men, for not keeping my mouth shut, and for using up all his coffee. Still I go on, telling them about the crops my grandfather tends, about our dogs, who are leaping onto their laps and sniffing their gold rings, as if they're just as hypnotized as I am by their splendor. Even the night nurse stops sweeping in the kitchen to join in on the conversation, though nobody can hear her, being soft-spoken, with a voice as small as a housefly. I can hear my grandmother now, yelling about how this is her house and she has lived here her whole life and has never once been invited out to dance at the parties of that rich puto and now she is dying and those parties are for those who wish to be first in line to hell. Just then, the man with the thick eyebrows takes out his rifle and yells at everyone to shut up, goddammit, just stop talking!

By now I gauge the time to be past five o'clock on some day around the first of this year, and the guerrilla soldiers are itching to leave. It's a new year, and we must be going, the man with the raised rifle says. We have business to attend to. He points the gun at me, at the night nurse, and then at my grandmother's closed bedroom door.

I stand up. I want to join them and see the world as they do: the swooping landscapes almost bursting at the seams with life, the open air, the hills and jungles so often covered in fog that I cannot imagine what sorts of creatures or people live out there without seeing them up close myself. These men might have the things I want, hidden in their suits or in campsites just over the mountain. I imagine feasts in the jungles. I imagine shooting their ammunition into the skies.

My grandfather should be coming home soon. I beg them: I want to celebrate the new year. Can't I come with you?

The night nurse grabs my arm, shaking her head and whispering something that sounds like a flutter of wind, dying and worthless. But it's too late; I've already planted the idea. The guerilla soldiers look at me with that same hungry look from before, and I smile. They grab my shoulder and lead me out of the house, leaving my grandmother screaming in her bedroom, saying something that for the first time I am able to ignore.

Outside, surrounded by guerrilla soldiers, I feel protected, like I'm inside a tank. We hike down my hill, and I feel we're a team, the way we're walking. I keep step with theirs and I watch our feet move—we're a single living thing, a beetle or a centipede, a thing with so many legs. My yellow rainboots and their black combat boots. Nearing the bottom of the hill, we stomp through a bunch of butterflies that had been resting in a heap of grass. Watching them burst into the air around us in a frantic flurry, it's like we made them blow up. Something inside me feels like counting, like yelling. When I get a gun, I'll shoot them through and through. Watch their wings fall to the ground.

I realize we're approaching the landkeeper's house. Up close, it's even bigger than I had expected. The adobe-tiled roof tilts at a sharp angle toward the grassy field, and its large windows are lined up in rows, three stories up. The music gets louder, and the people celebrating become silhouetted in the windows like puppets. To make conversation, I ask the guerrilla soldiers if they like dancing, but none of them respond. Their faces are stiff and they stomp through the field like they own this land, but they don't.

Although this land belongs to the landkeeper, I still feel a sense of ownership over it, since I have lived in these pastures and walked through these trees my whole life, which might not seem very long for somebody like a guerrilla soldier but for me it's everything I've ever known. Now, walking with the soldiers, I see it transformed. I can finally understand why the trees grow at certain angles and why the fences are placed where they are, though they are broken, trodden on by cows and passersby. I picture it through the eyes of someone conquering territories, and pick out the trees I'd want to keep as my own. When we reach the entrance to the house, it almost feels like a home I have owned for many years but have never had time to visit. I push my chest forward and raise my chin like women do when they are proud, and I walk through the front doors, letting the music swallow me up.

Inside, the narrow hallway opens to a living room full of people. I wave at them and imagine myself saying, Hello, my country, my people, hello. The music is so loud that nobody would even hear me anyway, so I scream and laugh and say strange words, and they all just keep dancing. I recognize some of the partiers as the hostages who had come by my house yesterday. They are dancing with other people who also look like escaped hostages, women with red cheeks and hair matted to their foreheads, clothes like rags and blotched with dirt. The walls are covered in portraits and paintings of the strange beasts that live in these mountains. The room is full of other treasures too, gilded decor and old books, though certain sections of it seem bare and sad. I wonder if I notice these gaps because I know something is missing. To anyone else, it might look as if nothing has happened here at all.

There's a band in the corner near the window, one with a drum between his knees, another singing while playing the accordion, another playing the guitar. Cumbia fills the room and people cheer. As I clap along to the music, I feel myself being pushed into the crowd. I look around, and realize it's the guerrilla soldiers who have pushed me. They have spread out along the perimeter of the room, guns raised at all of us. The one with the thick eyebrows yells at me, Dance, puta, dance.

Fine, I say, I like dancing anyway. And it's true. I learned to dance in my butterfly basement. It happened on my birthday, the last year we celebrated it. I wanted everything that I could sense outside the bounds of these acres of green, green land, but that day all I received was a cake with a single candle stuck in its center. I looked at it and it made me want so many things I couldn't even begin to name them. But then, like some instinct I never knew I had, all I wanted was to destroy the things that actually belonged to us. I reached for the cake. I still remember their looks of horror as I held it aloft in the dim light of the kitchen, and the way the frosting left prints like trodden rose petals on their shirts. I tasted the sweetness of the frosting on my fingers, then spit it out at their faces. The night nurse, who cannot stand the look of food that has already been chewed, shivered in her frock.

I went into the living room and started ripping out the stuffing from the couch, because I had seen the dogs do it and I wondered how it felt to rip something at the seams and let the insides burst out. The feeling made me want to sing, and I did. *La vida es un carnaval*, I sang, *Hay que vivirla cantando!* I could barely hear my grandfather's voice as I began throwing the yellow balls of stuffing around the living room, as though in celebration, until he opened the hatch to the basement and threw me inside. I was locked in there for days, or what seemed to be days, according to the number of thoughts I was having before I lost count. The butterflies flapped around my body, making little tornados of air, blowing my hair around my face. The basement, the disorienting darkness, the unmarked passage of time, made me question my grandfather, this life in our house on the hill, and why I felt compelled to celebrate. But after a long while, in the darkness where I could barely see my own hand in front of my face but where I could hear the rhythmic humming of the butterfly wings, I began to move unknowingly to the beat of their flight. I felt my rib cage pivot around my spine, my hips begin to sway. Days may have passed, but it felt as though it could still be my birthday, and my intuition was telling me that what I was doing was dancing.

I look at the people around me, who are now turning away from their dance partners and looking up at the men, who are pointing their guns at us. The music falters, but a soldier yells at them to keep playing, so they do. I can see now that there are more guerrilla soldiers occupying the house than the rest of us. It seems more soldiers have trickled in since I arrived. I look in the corner of the room and see a man wearing the kind of clothing I always imagine city folk wear, with a scarf wrapped neatly around his neck. I realize that it's him, the landkeeper. He, like the guerrilla soldiers, seems to shine with gold on different parts of his body—his glasses, his teeth, the buttons on his coat. The guerrilla soldiers have backed him into the corner with their rifles. The soldiers make the man look like he doesn't own this house, this land, but he does. He, like the rest of us, gets pushed onto the living room dance floor. Dance, they tell him, dance like the others. Passing around bottles of beer, the guerrilla soldiers say between swigs, We will have order!

They think they have us prisoners. Music is playing and we are dancing because that is what we have to do, but don't they know that this is what we have always done during New Years, when we know something will happen to us that changes the way we live our lives? The forward pushing of time, we feel it pressing inside our bodies. Come out, I want to tell it. We are ready.

I think about my house up the hill and my grandfather's basement full of butterflies, and my grandmother's fat that rolls over the edge of her mattress, threatening to anchor her to one place and time until she dies. I don't know how many thoughts I'm having and I can't tell how long I've been in the home of the landkeeper, but it must still be New Years, because nothing has happened to mark its ending. For now, we are stuck in the in-between of one year and the next. We are celebrating this moment, expanding it out toward even the hidden spaces in this valley, the fields where my grandfather works each day, my basement, filling all of it with our wanting. I'm at the party at the landkeeper's house wearing my nicest dress with butterflies still latched onto the hem. And around me are the guerrilla soldiers, and the men and women displaced from their homes who before this were walking toward a new life, a refuge. I wonder what it would be like to walk across this landscape now and see through the window that although people are being taken captive, they are still dancing and covered in butterflies, and if that's not reason to celebrate then I don't know what is.

Cristina Fríes is an MA student in creative writing at the University of California, Davis. Many of her stories explore ways in which women and girls contend with displacement and placelessness, disorientation, and trauma. Traveler and nomad at heart, she splits her time writing in California and Latin America. She is currently at work on a collection of stories and an opera. More at cristinafries.com.

EDITOR'S NOTE

Lin King's "Appetite" was published by *Slice* magazine in our Emerging Voices feature, which is part of our ongoing effort to connect the voices of established writers with authors who are just getting their start in the publishing world. King's story grabbed us immediately with matter-of-fact and yet powerful details that add up to a life—a scrawny body, a favorite song, pastries for breakfast, a dutiful embrace. King's Mayling is the only daughter from a well-to-do Taiwanese family who must choose a husband after a luncheon of small talk and commence with a life of duty and fulfilling expectations—clutching at and then letting go of any hope of passion or meaningful human connection. The life that Mayling is given is, as King writes, "as fair an offer as any twenty-four-year-old only daughter had reason to expect." In the span of five thousand words, King depicts the way in which an entire life, from childhood to motherhood to the wrinkles of old age, can be both perfectly acceptable and also utterly tragic in its emptiness. King's telling is unsentimental, and Mayling's life flashes by as briskly for the reader as it does for Mayling herself. The "appetite" of King's title is Mayling's persistent, barely acknowledged hunger for a different, more passionate existence, a hunger that threads through the back of the story without ever bubbling to the surface.

Elizabeth Blachman, editor in chief

Slice

APPETITE

Lin King

Wu Mayling never knew the pains of dieting. She had always been thin and pale. When she was a child, this had caused her nurse much anxiety, especially when other women would pinch Mayling's spare cheeks and shake their heads in disapproval. As a teenager, her scrawny figure led her mother to accuse the nurse of undernourishing Mayling. How will she ever find a husband, she cried, with those bony hips?

The nurse was dismissed, and her paychecks used to hire a new cook, a man with a formidable waistline and a head like a monk's. He was ordered to make pig feet stew once a week and chicken broth twice a week. But despite his best efforts, Mayling's body remained lean. The nutrition had to go somewhere, however, and instead of cushioning her bones it seeped inside them, making her taller than her mother and, in time, even than the cook.

In the fall of 1969, Mayling left her home in the south to attend the Teachers College in Taipei. Her mother had ordered the maid to sew cotton padding into the linings of her dresses to soften Mayling's harsh edges. By the time of her graduation, however, Mayling was wearing new, unpadded dresses that she had purchased with her allowance. A few of the dresses were even sleeveless, and these she hid in the bottoms of her suitcases, safe from parental discovery.

Still, the line had to be drawn somewhere, and despite her diploma-boosted confidence and head full of Carly Simon lyrics, Mayling did not own any denim.

She taught for just three years, at a private junior high school just outside Taipei. These were quiet years. She spent half of her weekends taking the bus to the city for movies and Western tea, and the other half in her small, spotless teachers' dormitory room, humming to records she'd bought herself with her more-than-adequate salary. She began learning to apply makeup by studying glossy magazines. On the longer holidays, she went home to lists of potential suitors, each one carefully evaluated and ranked by her mother: family friends, friends of family friends, optometrists, patent lawyers, accountants, chemical engineering PhDs.

Mayling met these young men at supervised lunches, always in the company of the suitor's mother and perhaps a couple of aunts. Some of the men were good-looking but mostly mute, never saying a word without direct prodding. Then there was the opposite breed: loud, garrulous, prone to excessive eye contact, desperate to dazzle. These candidates sometimes later telephoned her or wrote her letters at school, to which she responded briefly, out of obligation, never revealing much. Most of the men were quickly discouraged; those most impressed with themselves hung on for a little longer.

The third year of Mayling's life as a teacher, the year of her twenty-fourth birthday, her mother demanded that she choose a husband by the end of the Chinese New Year break. You'll have five months to get to know each other before getting married when the spring semester ends, she said. This being as fair an offer as any twenty-four-year-old only daughter had reason to expect, Mayling nodded her consent.

Three weeks later, she made her choice. His name was Wu

Shutian, a twenty-seven-year-old dentist in a steady, third-generation family practice. His main draw for Mayling, on paper, had been the location of his office, on the west side of Taipei, where fashionable theaters and shops lined the streets like paintings on display. During her college days, Mayling had frequented this colorful gallery borne of Taiwan's commercial boom, marveling at its glossy, motley charms. However dull her married life, she told herself, at least it would be lived in a place that was anything but dull.

In person, Shutian was decidedly a catch. He was tall, towering over his mother at a respectable 179 centimeters, with broad shoulders to match. He had a healthy complexion, thick eyebrows, and small eyes, which without his wire-rimmed glasses—as Mayling discovered later—gave him a somewhat comical look. When he had bowed his first greeting, Mayling's mother had tightened her grip on Mayling's forearm, signaling excited approval.

After a luncheon of small talk, the mothers had proposed that the young people take a walk in the nearby garden. They were old women, they'd said; they would stay indoors and have some more tea.

Mayling and Shutian trudged off stiffly together. When they reached the garden, safely out of their mothers' sight, Shutian's wide shoulders relaxed a little, and he stuck his hands in his pockets. Mayling said nothing. Shutian began to whistle.

Rainy days and Mondays always get me down, Mayling sang softly as he reached the end of the verse, her tongue slightly uneasy with the weight of the foreign words.

You know the Carpenters? he asked.

Yes, I've been buying their records since college, she said, looking at her kitten-heeled feet, which hurt.

Me too. I bought their newest one just last week, he said.

That evening, Mayling's mother announced to Mayling's father that she had at last found a husband for their daughter.

Mayling and Shutian were married in July, with a costly banquet and many blessings. They were not unhappy at their wedding. In fact, each was genuinely satisfied with their choice of the other. Their eyes were not offended by the faces they had vowed to look at for the rest of their lives; their hearts were fond of the same music, popular songs imported from England and America with which they would fill their home—songs their future children would soon tire of but nevertheless feel obliged to play at their parents' funerals.

On their wedding night, Mayling took a long bath while Shutian prepared tea in the kitchen. She could hear him pacing outside the door when she turned off the tap. After her bath, and a moment's hesitation, she decided to put back on the brassiere she had worn all day under her wedding dress. She then slipped into a white crepe nightgown that her mother had ironed herself and that was so crisp it crackled. It had a touch of lace trimming on the hem and a thin white ribbon that Mayling now tied into a bow at her collarbone. In the half-fogged mirror, she reminded herself of a heroine from a Gothic novel: her dark hair coiled in a damp braid, her face washed of rouge and powder, her waifish bone structure prominent under her thin, white gown.

When the newlyweds crawled under the thick duvet they now shared, they each had a rather morbid vision of what must happen, though neither was sure exactly how.

Shutian began kissing Mayling on the mouth. Her lips felt very thick and clumsy. She tried opening her mouth as she had seen kissers do in countless Hollywood films, if only to stop the swelling sensation in her lips. The texture of Shutian's tongue reminded

Mayling of the grilled pig's liver dish from their wedding banquet, and she wondered what hers might be reminding him of. Then, without warning, his tongue grazed the ridges of her front teeth, an act so alarming that she drew herself away from him sharply, moving back and back until her neck touched the headboard.

They did not try any more kissing that night, but through sheer biological instinct, Shutian managed to complete the act for them both. When it was over and he had fallen into a noisy slumber, Mayling wondered if it would hurt less in the future and whether she would ever experience the pleasure that Shutian had exhaled so heavily into her face.

With the red envelopes they had received from the wedding guests, they bought new clothes and furniture to fill the spacious apartment that Shutian's father had bought for them. They lined their new shelves with alphabetized soft-rock albums, Shutian's records to the left of the brand-new wood-framed Sony television, Mayling's to the right.

In the mornings, Shutian would pick out a record to go with breakfast while Mayling laid out the unchanging spread: sweet buns from the bakery down the street, hot coffee, and fruits of the season—mangoes, watery peaches, prickly lychees. With the constant presence of music, the lack of conversation in their home was not so apparent.

Mayling never visited Shutian at the dental clinic, though it was only one block from the apartment. She preferred to do her housework slowly, in between languid hours of sifting through records, skimming translations of foreign novels, and putting on makeup just to go grocery shopping. This way, when Shutian told her about his day or about the latest goings-on in the field of dentistry, she could be genuinely interested, if only for the novelty of the information.

Ten months after the wedding, to everyone's great delight, Mayling's tenure as a new bride was cut short when she attained the status of an expectant mother. The joy of both families was greatly multiplied when she gave birth to twins: a boy, Yijie, and a girl, Yixin. This was called a dragon-phoenix birth, one of the rarest and most coveted of good fortunes. With this extraordinary blessing, Mayling fulfilled her duties as a wife and daughter by producing, in a single afternoon, children of both the desired number and genders.

And motherhood bestowed upon Mayling yet another blessing: unprecedented beauty. The body that her mother had failed to create through excessive feeding now bloomed into being. Even after her stomach had flattened, a shapely fleshiness remained. In the street, she would examine her reflection in shop windows: now, instead of emphasizing her hollows and sharp angles, her knee-length cotton dresses revealed gentle, womanly curves. Clasping the hands of Yijie and Yixin, Mayling walked the streets with her head held high.

When the twins turned thirteen, they were plunged into their studies in preparation for the high school entrance exams. They took off at sunrise and did not come home until dusk, at which point they would practice their instruments for an hour—Yijie on the violin, Yixin on the piano—until Shutian returned from the clinic. The family would have dinner together, followed by an hour of playtime for the twins. After this, a young tutor, a recent graduate of Mayling's alma mater, would come to guide them through their homework and administer additional exercises until it was time for their baths.

Mayling found herself with an abundance of unstructured time, as she had in the first year of her marriage. Unused to this freedom, she had difficulty devising a routine that did not leave her taking several naps a day. Shutian proposed that she take up a hobby—what about guitar lessons? She liked the idea. Interest in music was one of the few things the two of them shared genuinely, not simply out of conjugal duty. She was thirty-eight, a perfectly reasonable age for learning a new trick or two. With the best possible education filling up her children's timetables, Mayling threw herself into her own second career as a student with a Yamaha beginner's model and a lengthy list of nostalgic ballads whose chords she hoped to master.

Declining Shutian's offer to hire a home tutor, Mayling signed up for private lessons at a music studio four blocks from their street. The boulevards of West Taipei had grown ever more kaleidoscopic in the thirteen years she had been busy raising her children, and she inhaled everything with the eagerness of a freshly weaned cub.

He asked her to call him Liang. This was what everyone at the studio called him. She was not sure if this was his given name or just part of it, or only perhaps a nickname. He told her his last name once, on the very first day of class, but she had not particularly cared to know it at the time and never found the opportunity to ask him again.

Liang was in his mid-twenties. In truth he could have been younger or older, but in Mayling's mind he was twenty-six. Everything about his face was petite and angular. He had narrow eyes, a small nose, thin lips, and a notably pointy chin. Even his ears were bony, a fact she noticed only because of his earrings—five silver hoops through the thin cartilage of his left ear. On any other man his face would have looked rather mouse-like, but these diminutive features were somehow balanced by his hair: thick, wavy curls—permed, she thought, though she never asked about this either—that he brushed to the right side of his head, emphasizing the piercings on the left. His unfussy wardrobe consisted of gray, white, and black T-shirts and faded jeans. He wore his keys on a long chain around his neck.

Mayling paid painstaking attention to Liang's appearance because it was the only thing she could take from him without anyone noticing. He was neither a great teacher nor a bad one. They began with C, E minor, G, D, A, A minor. She had great difficulty with F. He demonstrated on his own guitar, brushing her fingertips to make slight adjustments. A little more curved, he would say. Press harder, but don't squeeze, *press*. Twice a week she paid him five hundred Taiwanese dollars to soak in his scent of tobacco and laundry powder and, curiously, a hint of vanilla ice cream. His face was sunburned, even though it was the tail end of autumn. How? she wondered. She looked, and wondered more. The shape of his throat. The curve of his nose. The freckles on the backs of his hands. Did he sleep with another body at night?

She wondered.

At home, Mayling watched the man to whom she had given her life. Shutian, meanwhile, continued living his routine without ever noticing her gaze: reading newspapers at dinner, picking his ears and then sniffing the sullied finger, changing the television channel without asking, wriggling his strangely long gray toes while guffawing at political talk shows, requesting endless beers and endless massages. The beers distended his soft stomach and the backs of his arms and the skin under his chin. The massages forced Mayling to dig her fingers into these growing mounds of pillowy flesh. She felt them appear and expand in all the expected (and some unexpected) places on his body. On one of his birthdays, he received a bottle of cologne from his mother. He began dousing himself every morning, leaving pungent traces in the sheets, in the furniture, in the children's hair—even in the food on the table. Why did he never buy new records anymore?

In the studio, Mayling learned bits and pieces about Liang: he owned a black dog with a single white paw (he showed her a Polaroid), he had attended the University of the Arts but received very poor marks (he confessed with a laugh when she pointed out his memorabilia keychain), he loved guavas (he almost always ate one before class), he hated Coca-Cola. But that's a secret between you and me, he told her. He was full of little surprises like that, hinting at confidentiality when she did not expect it, with an offhand grin. Every few lessons he would give her a compliment—something small, maybe about her new haircut or improvements in her strumming, and, twice, about her "glow." These she gulped down hungrily and later etched into her mind's schoolgirl diary, reenacting them whenever she had a moment to spare.

Sometimes, when puzzling over a chord or lowering her head to hide her blushing, Mayling would feel the tingling sensation of his gaze gliding over the buttons on her chest, the waistband of her skirt, her bare shins, the recesses of her ankles. Most of the time, when she looked up again, he would be focusing dutifully on her fingers. But sometimes she would catch his eyes flickering away. This happened so rarely, though, and so fleetingly, that Mayling questioned her own senses. But just in case, she began rubbing scented lotion on her wrists and hands—the only parts of her body that he sometimes touched. And whenever he did touch her . . . did his fingers tremble, or did he inhale more deeply, or . . . ?

Shutian never asked her about her lessons. If she offered to perform for the family, he would listen with a toothy smile and hum along. But, on the whole, he treated her learning guitar as if it were an incidental attainment, something that simply happened when she picked up the instrument.

Mayling would watch him lying in the folds of the bed they shared. His face, like Liang's, had thin, small features; but these were so different from Liang's, his body ever so different from Liang's body, from both Liang's true body and the body in Mayling's mind, the one that cooed as she pushed her hips deep into his, one of his hands gripping her thigh, the other holding her under her armpit, his thumb pressing into her breast. This was the image that came to her on certain afternoons while Shutian and the twins passed more productive hours elsewhere, when she ducked under the covers and pressed herself against her palm again and again until she and Liang converged in a mutual grunt of climax.

Once, about a year into their lessons, Liang asked her what her plans were for the night.

Television, probably, she said, making sure not to smile too eagerly, with an expression that tried hard not to say, *Unless you have something else in mind.*

He was playing at a show, he said. A small venue, something of a cross between a bar and a black box theater, and she would have free entrance and food and drinks as his—was he consciously trying not to hesitate?—guest.

And Mayling pictured it: the grime on the postered walls and the dimly lit faces exhaling boozy cigarette smoke, appraising her. What on earth would she wear? She would be seen as Liang's guest. To be known, by anybody, as Liang's *somebody.* She looked up at him; beneath his casual demeanor she discerned childlike anxiety. He was nervous. He had probably rehearsed this casualness. She resisted the urge to bury her face in the curve of his neck. Maybe in that dingy basement, maybe in that moment when he was sweating from an impassioned performance under the dim spotlight, he would find the strength to brush her thigh with a calloused, feverish hand.

Laughter sounded outside the classroom. Images from the evening before crashed into her thoughts: Yixin, tearful from bickering with her brother; Shutian's slumbering face, with its comically round nostrils expanding, contracting, expanding, contracting.

That sounds like a lot of fun, she said, and thank you for inviting me. But I need to be up early before the kids leave for school.

That night, Mayling turned to face the snoring Shutian. She thought: I could have left you. I could leave you. I could leave.

Then, one spring day, two and a half years after they first met, Liang said goodbye. He had signed on with a small record company to replace the guitarist in an up-and-coming band. It was nothing fancy, but he had liked the demos they'd sent him, and it would be good experience. She had been a top-notch student, he said. First class. He hoped she would pick up his album when it came out. He hoped she would keep playing the guitar.

Mayling stopped playing the guitar. She offered no explanation to her family.

Yixin and Yijie were both accepted to the top high school in Taipei. Each would go on to National Taiwan University, Yixin to study English and French and Yijie to study economics.

Having not one but two children at the best school in the country could be considered enough good fortune for two lifetimes. But the twins went even further. Yixin flew off to Cambridge to garner more literary degrees; Yijie got a high-profile banking job in Hong Kong. By the time Shutian retired at sixty-six, family businesses had edged toward extinction. The management of the clinic was taken over by a trusted employee.

Shutian's retirement was to be expected given his age, but came as a rude shock to Mayling nevertheless. She had grown fond of her solitude, taking hours to prepare simple lunches for herself, watching daytime TV dramas with rambling plots, strolling through the neighborhood streets and marveling at the young people who filled them. Her children had been kind enough to induct her into the world of modern technology: she learned to browse news sites and blogs, email long-lost schoolmates, and, most notably, watch videos. Before the internet, she had been able to follow Liang's band—now decades old and with a respectable following—only remotely, haunting the CD store in search of increasingly rare album releases. Now she was able to see him. She could actually watch him online, drawing her face close to the pixels where his fingers touched the strings; she could pause the video as the camera swept past him on its way to the lead singer. She would touch the screen with icy fingertips and feel them turn hot as her whole body warmed at the image of him.

And now, to have Shutian at home, sharing her days? What would he say about her aimless routine? He had not asked about the details of her day-to-day life since the twins were born. Would they now have to relinquish their mutual genteel obliviousness of each other? She could not bring him beers and give him massages all day long. What would they do to fill up their hours? What could they add—after almost four decades—to fill up their marriage?

They were each too old to adjust to new habits in the other, Mayling decided. She would not, could not see Shutian as anything beyond the tired face whose whims, uninspired jokes, and gurgling bodily functions strained her patience from dinnertime to bedtime. He was a scheduled disturbance in her quiet existence. What if he decided to pick up some unbecoming hobby, like . . . *waltzing?*

Before her fears had time to be realized, however, an X-ray of Shutian's left lung revealed a shadow. The earliness of the diagnosis meant that surgery and recovery were both possible. But the worry, the bewildering medical vocabulary, the long-distance phone calls to Yijie and Yixin, and the trips to the hospital now filled up Mayling's days.

Yijie and Yixin, visiting with spouses in tow, decided that the work was too much for Mayling alone—what if she fell ill as well? A home care nurse was hired, a brusque woman in her fifties with a baked complexion and a gaudy collection of short-sleeved button-down shirts. Her name was Nini, a name Mayling found too dainty for a woman with such big, rough hands, such a big, rough grin.

The twins had worried that Shutian would find Nini's presence an insult to his masculine pride—but no, he soon took to her. He had, as Mayling knew, a natural disposition to being nursed. Nini was there to assure his every comfort, be it fetching the remote control, preparing snacks, or singing at his request: coarse folk songs from the South, Japanese-style enkas in the Taiwanese dialect, Teresa Teng ballads with all the wrong lyrics. A favorite pastime of Shutian's was to watch television on the sofa with Nini seated on a low stool beside him, massaging his feet with her left hand and snacking on cashews with her right. This seemed to Mayling a highly unsanitary habit, but as it kept both of them quiet and out of her way, she never objected.

Once a day, as his only exercise, Nini took Shutian for a walk in the nearby park. Mayling would take that time to read, or take a long bath, or stretch out under the covers. Sometimes she tried to recreate the image of Liang, pulling up his concert videos on her smartphone, but the sheets smelled too thickly of Shutian's illness. The rippling pleasure never came.

Neither of the twins was able to make it home for her sixty-fifth birthday, so she settled for phone calls filled with the squabbling and bickering of her grandchildren. Nini had insisted on buying a cake, but she chose Mayling's least favorite kind, with artificial-tasting fruit slices and three layers of heavy, cloying whipped cream. Nini also insisted on singing, and she made Shutian sing as well. Mayling was coaxed into making wishes and blowing out candles. After these painful festivities, Shutian and Nini went on their daily walk. Mayling, wearied to the marrow of her bones, took the opportunity to slip into bed with her favorite of Liang's music videos. She settled into the familiar position. She was about to click play when she felt a lump of cloth at her foot.

Removing her earphones, she tugged out the foreign object from under the covers. It was a ball of black pantyhose, rolled and tangled in a way that could only mean they had been removed in a hurry.

Mayling had not worn black pantyhose since before she had given birth.

She pressed play on the video. The familiar frames flashed by, Liang's face among them: a second here, a second there. When it ended, Mayling got up, wound the earbuds around the phone, and made the bed.

Shutian, whose last bottle of cologne had long sat empty on their bathroom sink, who reeked of camphor and that special scent of those whose skin was undersunned; Shutian, who had not changed the style of his glasses since 1986; Shutian, who had stopped bothering to remove her top during intercourse when they reached middle age, who would keep his eyes closed as she lay with her nightgown bunched up at her waist and the bedsprings creaked at an unvarying rhythm. Who had stopped doing even that almost ten years ago. How could such a man be harboring extramarital hosiery in his sickbed?

Mayling grabbed her purse from the dressing table and stuffed the pantyhose inside. She walked at a perfectly unremarkable pace out the door, down the two flights of stairs, and out of the building. Once outside, she turned a few corners before coming to an old-fashioned, run-down coffee shop. Inside, the tables were a reddish wood that clashed awfully with the cedar chairs. The menu was written in an unsophisticated font on plain printer paper with a clip-art Victorian border. The coarse, garish cutlery reminded Mayling of Nini, of Nini's coarse, garish body, a body that must have pumped itself against her husband's God knows how many times.

She ordered a rose tea, but when it came she did not drink it. When the shrill, peppy pop songs proved too much, Mayling paid for her tea and left.

She considered taking a taxi and going to a friend's, or maybe to the airport and on to Hong Kong, on to England, making a pit stop at, say, Turkey, Sweden, somewhere completely alien.

In the end, she decided to go with the bus. Any bus. One that would take her away from this corner of the city that had consumed her entire life. Not so far that she would no longer recognize her surroundings; only far enough that she no longer had to recognize herself.

On her way to the bus stop, she came across two mailboxes: red for express, green for regular.

Mayling stopped. Behind her, a group of boys passed by, talking about girls in quacking pubescent voices.

She took the pantyhose from her purse and unrolled the legs. She folded the hose neatly into a square and slipped them into the slot of the green box. Clasping her bag close, she smoothed the front of her dress and continued on to the bus stop.

Lin King grew up in Taipei and currently does most of her writing on the New York City subway. A global citizen, she writes about global citizens. She works for the artist Cai Guo-Qiang and is a graduate of Princeton University. See lin-king.net.

EDITOR'S NOTE

The editors of *The Baltimore Review* were drawn to "1983" for its quietly compelling story, the fine and often poetic quality of the writing, and the skillful weaving of a woman's personal story with details of this time of economic and political strife in Ghana. And what powerful and precise details—from the Harmattan fog and orange stars; to pots filled with boiling water and rocks to convince children their hunger will be satisfied; to Ghana-Must-Go bags; to a family curse; to a mother and daughter who are strangers to each other, and the only sound in the room a spoon grating against an earthenware pot.

The story mixes the ordinary stuff of life with mysteries, grittiness with magic. After the final page, we can't know with any certainty what the future holds for these women, but we can't help hoping for reconciliation and a better life for them. I think it takes considerable talent for a writer to do so much in a short story, and I look forward to reading more stories by Elinam Agbo in the future.

Barbara Westwood Diehl, senior editor
The Baltimore Review

1983

Elinam Agbo

IF NOT FOR the white Harmattan fog and the orange stars hovering over my eyes, I would have recognized Efua Agbezuge on the gravel road. Instead I squinted at the undulating shape, a dark vertical line with a glow, a full-body halo. It was a thirsty morning in December. Around the shimmering figure, hibiscus petals fell like slabs of shriveled flesh. The spiny remains of a rosebush snarled at anyone who passed it. No roosters crowed.

I was returning from a pond deep in the woods, where I occasionally found fish. I had not had any success in days and was wondering if I would need to try even earlier tomorrow. The sky turned from indigo to tangerine during my trek home, and daylight shone on my soiled hands and feet. I saw Efua—or rather, the shape of her—when I looked up from scraping the mud off my sandals. I immediately thought her a spirit and veered my wheelbarrow through a forgotten farm to avoid the encounter, trampling over cornhusks and cassava sticks. I was too disappointed to be haunted by an angel, too weak and empty to be bothered by a ghost.

I arrived at my doorstep to find items that had not been there earlier: a traveler's Ghana-Must-Go bag, a newspaper-wrapped tuber of yam, a small sack of gari. They looked so purposefully placed, leaning casually against the cracked clay of my hut. I had done nothing to deserve them—and yet there they were, at least two different kinds of food. I told myself it was another vision, induced by my hunger, fueled by false hope. What if my mind had conjured food in place of what may have been a bundle of snakes? There was no one around to tell me the truth, so I did not dare touch a thing. Either Tasi Mary had returned from Lagos, or my time was near.

THE YEAR WAS 1983 and no clocks struck anything except the hour of exile. Nigeria had begun its purge of our people—illegal immigrants, they were calling the Ghanaians seeking asylum from economic and political strife. The radio at Chief Ega's house wouldn't stop chattering about the millions congesting border checkpoints. Soon the returning exiles flooded the cities, crowding streets and diminishing resources. Food stores were drained as demand exceeded supply. Those of us who lived off the land were fine until the rains stopped and then the land rejected us too.

Here at home, the northeasterly wind blew dust in our faces. Neighbors visited less frequently. Probably because they couldn't stand one another's groaning. Some preferred to bide their time indoors—waiting for the arrival of rain or death, whichever came first. Others like Chief Ega, our resident rich man, seemed to have evaporated into the air. He had left no evidence as to where he had been or where he was going. Even the diligent kerosene boy was nowhere to be seen, leaving us to resort to lighting fire with dried palm chaff and twigs, the way we did before kerosene.

Rolling my empty wheelbarrow through our abandoned market, I could not help but reflect on how lonely the village roads had grown as burial grounds were prepared for the dying. No drums were pulled out for the dead. Rocks clanged in blackened pots, boiled all day to keep hungry children expectant until their eyes closed from fatigue. The last playful child I'd seen had stumbled on one of these pots, knocking it over and discovering his parents' ruse. I remember how abruptly his giggling had transformed into wailing, the pain of his burns inseparable from that of wretched disappointment.

Now even wailing required too much energy. Now those children who could still crawl out of their rooms went to Ane Afi, my grandmother, for her Anansi retellings, for tales she wove as deftly as the trickster-spider-man wove his webs. Before each story, the old woman would instruct her audience to break open dried palm kernels with rocks so they could ease their empty stomachs. I marveled at the strength in Ane's voice, how it carried, especially from a body surviving on koko with palm kernels in the morning and palm wine in the evening. As if porridge, nuts, and wine were enough to sustain her brittle bones. When I asked for her secret, she claimed to have experience with famines with the same air she claimed to have experience with storytelling.

As I reached the jacaranda tree in Chief Ega's compound, Tasi Mary's name escaped my cracked lips. I had been waiting for my aunt since news had reached me that her letters were lost in transit. There was nothing I could do but wait. Few lorries left the closest station and fewer arrived. We hadn't seen a new face in months. No merchants or cowherds. Ane Afi kept asking about the shepherd boys from neighboring villages whenever she craved meat.

I spent my days strolling through the village grounds and nearby forests, collecting palm kernels to deliver to Ane and searching for streams or ponds, because where there was water, there could be fish. On my way back, I would stop at Chief Ega's veranda, where he had left his wireless radio. I would replace the batteries when they ran out. I needed a reminder that there were still communities alive in the world.

Unfortunately, Chief's radio was stuck on one station, replaying the same news, but I listened to the crackling noise when the village lost its music. Also the radio of my mind was broken, on repeat, like the chorus of a song: Tasi Mary is not coming back. I had returned for Tasi Mary, but Tasi Mary would not return for me.

I needed something to break the loop.

"WHAT ARE YOU doing, Adzo?" my grandmother called. The resurrection of my day name broke through the sour song.

"I'm just sitting, Ane."

"Just sitting or inviting spirits into that head of yours?"

"I'm waiting for Chief," I lied.

Chief Ega was not really my older brother's name. I told myself the hunger had taken any memory of his given name so my inner jester could invent a nickname. (*Ega* I formed from *ga*, "money"). He had come to his wealth quite surreptitiously, from a bargain with an unnamed merchant in the Ashanti Region. Though I wondered: what if his road to affluence only seemed surreptitious to me?

"Oh, you didn't hear?" Ane said. "Your brother has abandoned us-oh."

From the glint in her eye, I knew Ane did not really mean her words, that she was aware of her grandson's whereabouts and did not feel at liberty to disclose it. She had always been our best secret-holder.

"Isn't running away what we Gameli children do best?" I played along.

"Ah, if only it was just the children," Ane started.

She slipped into the tale she always spun when discussing our family misfortunes. She started from the first Gameli who defied the odds and married the village beauty, a taciturn young woman with eyes black as obsidian and skin soft as feathers. The bachelors had been seeking the beauty's hand since her first blood, and while the men seemed blind to her lack of status—she was an orphan—the women of the village grew suspicious of her vague origins. Some suggested she was the wife of a river god in her previous life, hence her charms. Others claimed she carried an ancestral curse, hence her solitude. The men, perhaps because they were enchanted, dismissed these rumors and envied Gameli his fortune. For that is what she brought him—weeks after the wedding, Gameli happened upon a diamond in a stream, then another, and another. Even the wise elders could not explain his sudden prosperity. The women began to think maybe Gameli's marriage was not a curse but rather a boon.

Even if it was a boon, time revealed it to be an ephemeral one. His wealth amassed in cattle and farmland for years until it became clear that Gameli's wife could give him diamonds but not children. No longer a young man, he hoped to leave his riches to a son. He sought counsel from his peers and elders, who advised him to take another wife. This is when the invisible thread of his bride's silence snapped. That moonlit night, the villagers heard a loud cry and saw a blazing trail of fire, from Gameli's compound into the forest. Months passed and no one heard from either Gameli or his wife. One day, the man appeared with a baby boy and no wife. Whatever happened in the depths of that forest had stripped him of his memory. Such was the origin of an affliction that would linger in his bloodline for generations to come.

WHEN ANE FINISHED, she leaned her cane against the wall and sat a step below me. I released a broken breath. I had heard this story many times. It was the reason I left for the capital at sixteen, in search of answers that were not hidden in lore. Answers that would lead me to a cure and a future.

"Ane, what does that story have to do with Chief?" I asked, to keep her talking.

"Oh, child," she said. "It has to do with everything in our family."

Her ensuing silence sent me back into the halls of my mind.

I used to believe in curses. In womanhood, however, I felt emptied of faith regarding blessings and curses alike.

At least one child in our family contracted Gameli's affliction every generation. Sometimes the symptoms were mild, as it was with Ane, whose mental lapses did not hamper her life—she raised nine children and was respected for her wisdom. But there were also cases like my mother, who, like the first Gameli's wife, wandered into the forest, never to be seen again. The elders told me her dark eyes had been wild that morning, rolling around in search of a fixed point to latch on to. They said she had not recognized anyone's face, not even my father's, and by the time they thought to restrain her, it was too late. She was gone.

Tasi Mary shared my distress—she had holes in her mind too. When I became a woman and informed her of my plans, she paid for my passage to the capital. I arrived in the city before realizing that answers did not grow on trees. They were held in books and those books were locked in towers I could not reach. I needed to eat and so I searched for work. With my primary school English, I became a nanny for a private school teacher who later recommended my services to her employer, a white woman named Hannah. To join her household staff, I was baptized into Hannah's faith—at the time, the sprinkling of water on my head seemed a harmless prerequisite for the coveted job. I raised Hannah's twins for four years. The girls clung so closely that their mother invited me to accompany her to England. Shocked, first by her willing detachment from the children, then by her recognition of my service, I asked for time to think on it.

A few weeks before Hannah needed my final answer, a hand gripped my shoulder as I was shopping for groceries. It was my brother, then a newly crowned chief. We embraced and addressed each other's health. I praised his brawn and his batakari, a smock he had won off a gambler from the North. He told me I had grown beautifully. Our pleasantries dissipated, however, when I shared Hannah's offer. He demanded I return home immediately—how could I even consider running off to some unknown land, the white man's land no less? His rage did not give room for my defense, and I did not get the opportunity to bid Hannah's girls farewell.

Back in the village, Tasi Mary was my sole advocate. Outside of Ane's tale, no one understood my reasons for leaving. Even surrounded by my well-meaning relatives, I felt drained of purpose, like an empty vessel that can never hold water. The elders asserted, in that resigned manner of the burdened, that life's questions often do not have clear answers.

While their words were validated by experience, my aunt and I—afflicted as we were—could not find peace in their truth. She arranged for me to marry Edwin Agbezuge, a city doctor whom she believed could find a cure for me, if such a thing were possible.

Less than three years later, I stopped recognizing my husband's face. I ran back home to an infuriated Chief and a departed Tasi Mary.

I WOKE FROM my thoughts to the sun receding beyond the horizon. I did not even remember Ane leaving her place on the steps. The only sign of her presence was the shawl around my shoulders. I walked home, considering whether a jug of palm wine would clear my mind. I moved the bags inside the hut, too weary for caution. I pulled out a stool and rested my back against the clay wall. I was placing a cool cloth on my forehead when the knock came.

"I'm looking for Rose," the person on the other side said. "Rose Gameli."

I raised a candle to see who was asking for me and saw eyes that mirrored mine. Eyes the color of dusk.

"I am she," I told the owner of those eyes.

"My name is Efua," she said. "Efua Anya Agbezuge. I'm your—"

"Child," I said, the word like the abandoned secret it was, a revelation I had never intended to hide. "You're my child, my daughter."

Her reply was a grave nod.

"Are you getting married?" I blurted, forgetting custom. No *come inside, sit down, what will you like to drink, and tell me of your journey*? my better half chastised. The opposing half, who was curt and brash, replied: *Why else would she be here?*

"I'm sixteen," Efua said, and I wasn't sure if that was a reply to the marriage question or the question I had asked myself.

A gust of wind rattled the plywood door. Efua shivered. I let her in. Normally I would request proper identification from a stranger but Efua's identification was in her eyes, her mouth, her nose. I presumed the long forehead came from her father, whose face I still could not recall.

"Are those yours?" I asked, pointing at the bags I had dragged inside.

She nodded. "They're gifts for you," she said.

Gifts. Gifts were for women who did not leave their two-year-olds crying on a dock, women who were not always looking for an escape from the future. Gifts were for mothers, and I had relinquished my motherhood fourteen years ago.

"Are you returning from Lagos?" I asked, because I could not confess my ruminations on gifts. And because Ghana-Must-Go bags, in those days, carried Nigeria's outcry for Ghanaians to go back to their country.

"I'm sixteen," Efua repeated. I suppose she felt that was all I needed hear in order to understand. As in, *I'm sixteen—isn't that too young to marry, too young to leave home for a foreign land?*

I wanted to tell this girl who wore my face that children younger than she had gone to Nigeria. Children like Chief's son who left at fourteen, against his father's wishes, to find his own path. I wanted to tell her she could not trust anything I said, since even the knowledge recorded in my journals came from other minds, those who remembered what I could not. I wanted to tell her sorry, that Tasi Mary was not here to offer the possibility of a more coherent truth. Sorry, for everything else.

Our eyes met for a moment—hers searching, mine avoiding—as I was thinking of the next thing to say. I swallowed, a lump that irritated my parched throat. I could not think of the appropriate words and felt a hot wave of shame; I was awkward and uncertain, like a child.

"Make yourself at home," I murmured finally. My eyes returned to the ground.

THE FOLLOWING MORNING, I opened my eyes to her face hovering above mine. I blinked in question. She withdrew, almost reluctantly.

Efua poured some gari into water, allowing the mixture to rise to make eba. I thought she was preparing her breakfast, but then she handed me the bowl.

"You don't have to do this," I said.

She shrugged and prodded me to eat with only her gaze. I succumbed and ate half, offering her the rest.

After breakfast, Efua braced her head on her palm. We waited for something neither of us knew how to initiate. Was it mother-daughter conversation or something more rudimentary? And where could we begin when I did not possess all of myself, and she could only know what others had said of me? We were both unreliable.

I left for my daily trek into the forest and returned at the close of day to find Chief Ega at my door. He was speaking to Efua.

"You are always welcome here, child," I heard my elder brother telling my forgotten daughter. This was the same man who had said, upon my return from a failed marriage, "What did you think would happen to a girl who went without her family's consent to marry a man named *Agbezuge*? Of course she will bring us his *belligerent life*."

At least there was some comfort in the knowledge that his frustrations did not extend to that *belligerent* man's child.

"Where's Tasi Mary?" I remembered to blurt out before he could vanish again.

"Dead to us," was all he said. *Like you*, I expected him to add, but then my mind lingered on his use of "us," to his crippled tone. I wanted to ask whether he was finally including me, but by then my brother had departed with the last light.

Later, when I browsed through the words in my journals, I would wonder if I had asked of his son, if he had shared that knowledge with me, if I had willingly left the answers out of my written memory.

THE NEXT DAY, we rose to the first rooster's crow. Before I could roll up my thatch-mat, Efua prepared breakfast and filled in my gaps. She had roamed the village for two days—first upon her arrival and then again when I left her in my hut the previous day. She had introduced herself as my daughter, interviewing those of my relatives whose doors remained open. Surprising myself, I asked if she had heard anything new about Tasi Mary.

"Chief said he traced her to the Southwest, where she had married a Yoruba man and bore three children," Efua said.

She pulled her stool next to my place on the mat. Her head cocked to the side as she peered at me through thick lashes.

I nodded, not just to satisfy her. I was relieved to hear my aunt continued to live even as I grieved the distance between us.

Efua took a deep breath then added, "He also said she did not remember him."

I looked up at her then, not expecting what I found. It was solace, however temporary, I saw in the swirling black inside the brown of her irises. She, at least, had discovered some of the truth she was seeking. Lips pursed in a sympathy I did not deserve, Efua gave a nearly imperceptible nod before turning to my cooking utensils. I studied her shoulder blades as they curved in and out. Imagining the focused frown she now hid from me, I listened to the grating of a spoon against an earthenware pot, the promise of a shared meal, of full stomachs and hearts warmed in homecoming.

If I had not known better, I would have thought the Harmattan fog was seeping through the space under the door, clouding my vision so I couldn't see where either of us would be the next day, the next year, or the years after that. But I knew better. I knew the girl sitting across from me was not a trick of the mind, that we were two strangers seeing each other for the first time.

Elinam Agbo moved to the United States from Ghana when she was ten and has since lived in Nevada, Kansas, South Carolina, and Illinois. She received her BA from the University of Chicago, where she won the 2017 Les River Fellowship for Young Novelists. She is currently an MFA candidate in the Helen Zell Writers' Program at the University of Michigan.

EDITOR'S NOTE

Ernie's piece initially came to our attention through a reader, who came upon it in Submittable and assured us it deserved a serious look. We were immediately struck by the graceful and relaxed manner in which this story is told; there is a confidence and an ownership in the voice that is extraordinarily compelling. Right from the start, the reader discovers a very dynamic and three-dimensional character in the narrator, one whose voice alone draws you onward. Throughout the piece, Ernie showcases a very sharp command of narrative timing: he has a great instinct of when a scene should end, when a scene should be teased, suspended, to be returned to later. All this creates a kind of river that carries you along as a reader, that breaks your heart over and over again. Ernie's is a voice that readers ought to listen to, which, on top of an impressive narrative command, is overflowing with tenderness and earnestness that couldn't be fabricated with any amount of literary might.

Claire Boyle, managing editor
McSweeney's

STAY BRAVE, MY HERCULES

Ernie Wang

THERE'S A TUG on my skirt. I look down.

"Hi there, young fella," I say.

"Hercules," he says.

I nod.

"I have a question," he says.

"Go on then, young man."

"Hercules," he says. "How do I become strong like you?"

I look at his parents. They beam at their son and smile like they already know.

We're at the corner of Frontierland and Fantasyland. From a distance, I hear screams at the top of Splash Mountain and calliope music from the riverboat making its way downstream. The smells of butter popcorn and churros wafting through the muggy afternoon air remind me that I'm hungry and I'll be on my break soon.

In the far corner, I see Buzz and Woody ham it up for a large Chinese tour group. Cameras click, and the tourists point and shout furiously at them. Buzz and Woody take it in stride and swivel randomly and wave enthusiastically and do this jiggy kind of dance. Today, Zac is Buzz. He's a good dude. He sees me, and without turning from the tourists, he lowers his arm and flips me the middle finger.

I kneel down and clasp the kid's hands. He stands straight and puffs out his chest. I no longer have to think back to the script. I got this shit on lock.

ALL OF DISNEY'S eighteen Herculeses have nicknames for each other; mine is Babyface Hercules. There's also Douchebag Hercules, NASCAR Hercules, the high school twins Juicehead and Jailbait, Born-Again Hercules, and everybody's favorite: Grandpa Hercules. Grandpa Hercules is literally a grandpa, and between shifts he brings out photos of his granddaughters in the breakroom, and we tell him they're beautiful, because we love him. Then one of the Jasmines or Snow Whites help him reapply his makeup, because he needs a shit-ton.

I've been Hercules ever since I dropped out of college to be with Jay. I would've come back even if he wasn't sick. But the night he called and matter-of-factly explained that it had spread to his lymph nodes and his testicles and brain, I immediately packed a backpack and left the Michigan snow and drove straight back to Florida.

Jay is thirty years older than I am. He had warned me when we first met that something like this might happen. Bodies break down over time, he had said.

On the drive back, I replayed his last words on the phone: *I am statistically unlikely to make it to the end of the year, but these standard deviations are large, as you might expect, Jeremy . . .* Jay always talks like that. He's an actuary, which surprises nobody.

When I pulled into his driveway that morning in yet another torrential Orlando rainstorm, my fuel tank empty and my eyes bleary and my breath reeking of gas station coffee, he walked out onto the driveway, his glasses fogged and dripping, his robe pressing into his gaunt frame as it absorbed the rain. He looked at me as if he was struggling for words, and then he said, "You just drove a little over twelve hundred miles, which by my calculations puts your average speed at—"

I flung myself onto him and kissed him. "Not fast enough," I said as I pulled him back into the house.

"I'm starving, let's grub," I said later as we lay in his bed. "And I'm done with this long-distance shit," I said. "And, I told my parents I'm moving in with you, and that you're not doing well."

He just kind of shook his head and looked sad.

The first thing I did after I moved in with Jay was look for a job. Aladdin and Gaston and Donald Duck train at my gym, and one day we were all talking by the water fountain, and they said they might be able to help. The next thing I knew, I was at Disney employment headquarters getting my head measured and my chest waxed under the watchful, glowering scrutiny of the casting director.

I got over myself and threw all my chips into this job. I mean, it's not awful, and at night, after Jay falls asleep, I hop online and look for other jobs, as I promised him I'd do. I get to the park an hour before my shift and they tell me where I need to be at and at what time and anything I need to be aware of. Then I get in line with the other cast members for makeup. I go to the locker room and change into costume. The casting director sometimes scrutinizes me—she calls it quality control—and checks me off on her clipboard. Then I'm out the door, squinting under the bright Disney sun. For the next three hours, I smile and hug and flex, and the best part is that I get to drop wisdom bombs on adoring crowds, even though my answers are limited to what's on script. Be strong and be brave, I say. Listen to your parents. They're not half bad.

During orientation, the casting director handed me a thick

binder filled with scripts to memorize so I'd know how to stay in character for every conceivable situation. Every catastrophe here is called a situation, and every single one is covered. If lightning strikes and fries a sixth-grade class, there's a section for that on what Hercules would do. When a soccer mom tries to kiss me on my lips I'm supposed to pretend to play hard to get and then try to distract her by shoving my muscles in her face. Hercules can be such a tease. Then when her husband tries to pick a fight with me, I'm supposed to pretend that we're actually play-fighting, and then I'm supposed to run and get out of there. Hercules can be a bitch. When a kid's being a jackass and asks a dumb question—this part I actually like—I'm supposed to twist his question into one that's more family friendly, and then from there I'll give one of my stock answers. In the end, it's all about staying on script and running and evading. I am a born natural at that.

THE BOY AND his parents stare at me expectantly.

"Hercules," the boy repeats. "How do I become strong like you?"

The scent of churros is slaying me, but this kid is adorable, so I squeeze his hands and gaze into his wide eyes.

"Young man, what's your name?"

He takes a deep breath and shouts, "Garen."

"Young Garen, I want you to be strong, I want you to be brave, and I want you to listen to your parents. Do you understand?"

Garen swivels and looks at his parents, who look this close to combusting with pride. They reach for each other's hands and nod and mouth the words *I understand, Hercules* at him.

Garen focuses his attention back toward me. He puffs his chest out again, and he shouts: "Dad wears Mom's dresses and makeup like you do."

When he sees me with my mouth agape, he attempts to clarify. "But only when Mom's not home," he assures me.

I know the absolute worst thing I can do in this moment is to look at Garen's parents, but that's what I do. Their hands are clasped, and their smiles remain plastered, but nothing registers in their eyes. It's like four vapid orbs gatewaying into an abyss. Then she shoves away his hand and turns to look at him, and it's like I can already see her about to say, *Honey, is that true?*, and I can already imagine him struggling to come up with some way to respond, and then I'm like, Nah this fool is so boned. And in this moment, the only thing running through my mind is, I'll be damned, that binder doesn't cover everything after all.

"THEY DON'T PAY us enough for this shit," Zac says. Zac and I are slumped in our chairs in the breakroom. We're still in costume.

In the far corner, Annabelle is having lunch with her daughter. In the past, as Ariel, Annabelle was legendary for how she connected with the kids. There would be a line of children with their parents snaking around the corner, patiently waiting to hug her and tell her about school and their pets. She would smile with delight and say, "Tell me more." Then Annabelle had her daughter. When she returned from maternity leave, she had put on a little weight, and they reassigned her to a new job as a fully covered Mickey. Her Mickey headpiece sits on the table as her daughter cries and says she doesn't like to be left with employee childcare. "I'm so sorry, sweetie," Annabelle says. She looks exhausted.

"So what did you say to that family?" Zac asks.

I shrug.

Garen's mom had marched toward us and was about to yank Garen away when I stood and gently held her hand.

"Ma'am," I said quietly.

She tried to shake my hand off. Her back and shoulders were as rigid as a springboard.

"Just let us go," she said, and her shoulders slumped, and I saw tears begin to well around her squinting eyes.

"Can I just say something real quick to Garen?" I asked.

She hesitated, and then she tightly nodded.

I knelt down and grabbed Garen's hands once again. He looked confused and as if he might cry too. I leaned forward and spoke directly into his ear.

"Young man," I said, and he whispered a tiny *yes* back.

"Hercules wants you to know," I said, "that no matter what happens, your dad and mom love you very much, okay?"

He nodded.

"So I want you to be brave, and I want you to be strong, and I want you to listen to everything they tell you, okay?"

He nodded again.

"And now," I whispered. "Hercules wants you to go give your mom and dad a big hug. Can you do that for Hercules?"

He nodded one last time, and he ran to his mom and hugged her tight, and he ran to his dad, who had been standing unsurely in the background. Then they were gone, and my shift was about over, so I stood and walked back to the breakroom.

I think for a moment. "I guess I stayed on script," I tell Zac.

He stares.

"I mean the script's not half bad," I say, and he nods and loses interest.

•

JAY LOOKS UP from his spreadsheets when I come home that night. His company lets him work from home, so most nights I find him surrounded by reams of paper. He doesn't let the cancer stop him from putting in a full workday, and he's meticulous about tracking his hours.

"How was your day?" he asks.

"It was a blast," I say. "Dads getting caught lying, and kids needing therapy for the next ten years."

"So just another Disney day?" he says.

"Yep. How was yours?"

He takes off his glasses and rubs his eyes before he reaches for a stack of papers and pointedly raises one.

"Jeremy," he says. "We need to talk inheritance and insurance. I've run some initial calculations, and the projections indicate . . ."

I tune out when he begins to use big words, but he gets more animated as he picks up steam on his findings, and he's sexy as fuck as he incessantly taps his paper with his pen, so I strip off my shirt and straddle him.

He stops talking.

"Ah," he says.

"Let's talk about your impending death some other time," I say.

Later, I step out of the shower and find Jay curled up on the sofa. His glasses, off-kilter, are hooked onto one ear and hanging on his forehead over wisps of his fine hair. He snores lightly. I stare at his face. When he's awake, he always looks as if he's worried about something, probably because he is. Worried about me, probably. He likely has months left, and the only thing he seems to have on his mind is whether I'll be okay after he's gone. It's only when he's asleep that he finally looks relaxed. He snorts, and traces of a thin smile begin to form. I wonder what he's dreaming about, and that makes me smile.

I WAS BACK home with Jay for summer break when we first learned about the cancer. By then, we had been together for two years. The prognosis was bright then, and Jay was adamant I return to college.

"I'll be cured before you come back," he said.

That night, needing to get out of the house, we went to P.F. Chang's.

"Are we celebrating anything special tonight?" our server asked.

"Just our health," Jay said gently.

"That's very sweet," the server said, smiling. She studied us, and she said, "Well you two look as healthy as—"

"It's my birthday," I cut her off. Her mouth curved into an O, and she said she'd give us a minute to look at the menu.

Jay turned and gave me his look.

"What? Health doesn't get you free cake at P.F. Chang's," I said.

"I suppose that's true," he said.

We were subdued for most of the dinner. It was toward the end, after dessert, that I could no longer hold back.

"What if things go wrong?" I blurted out. I was reeling from too many apple martinis.

"Jeremy," he said. "Do you realize, statistically, how many standard deviations off we need to be to see the treatment fail?"

I said nothing.

"It's a little under three," he said. "Expressed numerically, that equates to—"

"Okay. Okay."

He reached over for my hand and nodded.

"I'm going to be fine, Jeremy. You have to trust me, and you have to trust in the numbers."

I relented. In the darkened room, the candle flickered over his creases and reflected tiny orange flames in both lenses of his glasses. He's all lit up in fire, I thought. And I believed.

But I should have never left him.

EVERYBODY'S IN A shitty mood at the park today. This happens sometimes. Some days, with no reasonable explanation, foul moods spread and take over entire sections of the park like a contagion. By midmorning, under the already wilting sun, tempers flare within families and in groups of middle school friends, Tomorrowland's Space Mountain dome standing glumly in the backdrop.

This includes Cody, the eight-year-old bald-headed Make-A-Wish kid who's sitting in his wheelchair with his arms crossed. He glares as his parents stand helplessly to his side and as the swath of media photographers fumble with the cameras draped around their necks and do not take photos.

Cody's mom approaches him and places her hand on his frail shoulder. "Honey," she says, "is there anything we can do to make you happy?"

"I want to go home," he says, and the Make-A-Wish and Disney public relations people wince in unison.

"But sweetie," she says. "Isn't this what you wanted to do more than anything in the world? What changed?"

"Disney World sucks," he shouts, and I see two photographers quietly pack their cameras back into their cases.

Dad is starting to unravel, and I see him approach Cody with his fists clenched. Before I realize what I'm doing, I find myself standing between Cody and his dad, my face lit up in smiles. I motion subtly at his dad before I kneel down and face Cody.

"Hi there, young man. Your name is Cody, right?"

Cody stares at my biceps with wide eyes. My physique generally has that effect on most boys who regularly worship Marvel superheroes, and I can imagine that the effect is greater on a kid as sick as Cody. He nods and looks into my eyes shyly.

"Young man," I say. "I hear you on your discomforts. It's too hot and it's too crowded and everybody's in a bad mood."

He nods emphatically.

"So tell me," I say. "If you could do anything right now, what would it be?"

His face brightens. "Video games," he says.

I nod in complete agreement. I say, "Hercules loves video games. What's your favorite?" and he shouts, "Minecraft," and I silently sigh in relief. That's like the one game I have some knowledge of.

"That's Hercules's favorite game," I say, and he looks as though he might jump out of his wheelchair and hug me. "What are you working on right now?" I ask, and Cody smiles and closes his eyes for several moments, as though he had transported himself out of Disney and into his Minecraft world. When he opens his eyes, they are shining.

"I found a way that I can fly forever," he says.

I say, "Hercules wants to hear *all* about this." The photographers take their cameras back out of the cases, and as the cameramen begin to record from a distance, Cody explains to me in a feverish pitch and with two animated hands the mechanics and items he acquires before he sprints and dives off a cliff and launches himself higher and higher into an infinite horizon—eventually so high, in fact, he explains, that the game stops rendering his image, and he disappears entirely from the screen.

"That is very high," I agree. "But Cody," I say. "If you fly beyond the horizon and disappear, won't you miss your parents?"

"It's just a game, Hercules."

"Touché."

"Hercules?"

"Yes, Cody."

"I'm dying, you know," he says. From the corner of my eyes, I sneak a peek at Cody's parents. They stare intently at their son.

"I know," I say.

"Hercules?"

"Yes, Cody."

"Will you come to my home and play Minecraft with me?"

I say nothing.

"So we can fly forever?" he says.

I look into his eyes, and I can see that he is bracing for the inevitable no. "I have an even better idea," I tell him as I begin to smile. He looks up. "Peter Pan's Flight is a short walk from here. Have you been on the ride?"

He shakes his head.

"Hercules promises you," I say, "that riding that ride feels just like flying. How about we take that flight together, just you and me?"

He considers this for a moment before he says a quiet *okay.* I turn to his parents for permission, but they already look like they might throttle me with gratitude, so I stand and take Cody's hand as his mom pushes his wheelchair. Behind us, the photographers and media and public relations teams quietly follow, and the crowd ahead splits to make room when they see the procession. But I only have eyes and ears and heart for Cody—script be damned—and he has me eating out of his hands as he patiently explains master-level tips on how to rule over the Minecraft domain.

A PHOTO OF me kneeling and clasping a smiling Cody's hands makes the front page of the local newspaper the next morning, along with the caption "Local Hero Captures the Hearts of Boy and Disney Community." Jay lowers the paper and raises his eyebrows over breakfast.

"You sure work hard for nine dollars an hour," he says.

"They should promote me to management," I say crossly. I couldn't sleep last night.

"Or at least to playing Gaston. Now that's a real man," Jay says as he dodges the Cheerio I flick at him. He returns to the paper, and I get ready to leave for work.

The Orlando roads are slick with rain this morning, and the traffic is heavy. I'd always wondered why they chose to build the Happiest Place on Earth in practically the Wettest City in the Country. I like it when it rains, though.

I stare past the windshield wipers sweeping frenetically to keep my vision unobscured. Outside is a sea of gray. With every gust of wind, sheets of rain shimmer. Trees shudder.

I hear the approaching wail of sirens. I pull over and stare at the ambulance as it passes by and then turns at the intersection, in the opposite direction from home. I remain parked by the curb. The sirens fade, until I hear only the rain pelting the roof of the car and the furious beating of my heart. I rest my eyes and feel the heat radiate through my closed eyelids.

Yesterday, on Peter Pan's Flight, while waving a very temporary goodbye to Cody's parents and the media folk, I helped Cody step on board the suspended galleon that served as our flying ship. We settled in our seats and launched high into a dark London night. We flew over Tower Bridge and Big Ben before rising to clouds of wispy white fluff swaying under giant whirring fans made invisible behind the cloak of night sky. Below, a sea of tiny golden lights—villages of homes shining kerosene lanterns—twinkled and pulsed, as if the constellations lay not above us but below.

I looked at Cody. His face was spellbound as we glided and swooped over mountain peaks and into the heart of Neverland. At one point, our galleon dramatically lifted high into the sky to escape the wrath of an enormous crocodile. Cody whooped and wrapped his arms around me. I squeezed his shoulder and pointed down at the crocodile, who now held Captain Hook in the clutches of his jaws.

As we emerged outside and through the exit that led to the disembarking zone and to Cody's parents welcoming us back, Cody sighed and rested his head on my shoulder.

"How'd that feel, Cody?" I said. "Was that just like flying or what?"

He sighed again and embraced me and said, "That was way better than Minecraft." I squeezed him tight before I stood and helped him off the galleon and into his waiting wheelchair.

After insisting it was not a big deal to Cody's parents and posing for a final round of photos, I said my goodbyes and jogged back to my post in Tomorrowland. As I navigated between throngs of people making their way to their next attraction, I imagined that it had been Jay and I flying on the galleon. Jay, being Jay, would peer over the ledge and at the city below, and he'd squint and point out, "The placement of Big Ben seems off. It should be over *there*." I'd tell him to shut up and enjoy the ride. He would remain silent for a moment, and then he'd look up toward the ceiling and say, "The engineering in this facility is really quite remarkable, if you stop and consider—"

"Shut *up*," I'd say again.

I'd close my eyes and shiver when the cold air blew over my ears. In the distance, I'd hear Peter Pan and Hook's swords whirl and clang in battle as the Darling kids cheered and whistled. Jay would turn to me and pause and cock his head, and he'd say, "Is everything okay, Jeremy?"

And I'd grip the ledge so hard that pain shoots up my wrists, but he wouldn't see that, and I'd smile and say, "Yeah, just hungry. Let's get a turkey leg after this." And for the rest of the ride we would remain quiet, our galleon propelling us above a dark ocean and gliding toward the exit, where sunlight would peek in from around the corner and the cast members, bored shitless, would remind us to watch our step on our way out.

Ernie Wang resides in Las Vegas. He received his MFA in fiction from the University of Nevada, Las Vegas. His work is forthcoming in *The Threepenny Review* and *Passages North*.

EDITOR'S NOTE

The Rumpus strives to make space for writing that might not a find a home elsewhere. We love stories that build bridges, tear down walls, and speak truth to power. In "Bellevonia Beautee," Lauren Friedlander situates the reader within the characters' world but insists we leave all assumptions at the door. The story is full of detail but also mystery. Most importantly, this story pushes against tropes of women victims in fiction. The female victims here are granted agency and imagination. They are more vivid and fully fleshed out on the page than the man holding them captive. Their humanity is rendered with clarity, and they refuse to surrender to their circumstances in small ways, and ultimately, perhaps, in not so small ways.

Marisa Siegel, editor in chief
The Rumpus

BELLEVONIA BEAUTEE

Lauren Friedlander

Every morning Andrew fetches her breakfast. This is just a recent thing. I've seen him reading in a book that it is vital to treat your woman kind. Something special at least every day, a little surprise to keep everyone on his or her toes. So for Deb especially, he treks down the mountain in the early hours, when dawn is on the brim, all violet, and he hits up the diner that is like a half mile east, maybe less, called Cassidy's. Cassidy doesn't work there anymore—she's passed—but new customers always ask. I haven't been let down to Cassidy's in a bit. I remember they had nice red booths with glitter in the vinyl or something that made them sparkle.

I stay put in our tent with Deb. I stay put and Andrew goes "hunting." I am fully aware that this is the way it's been done between man and woman for eons now, and my mom used to say there's no need to fix what hasn't broke.

Deb prefers eggs, scrambled, and toast cut into triangles with butter pats and grape jelly on top. It takes Andrew a full hour at least to get all the way down the mountain and all the way east to Cassidy's, so by the time he is back, the food's gone cold. The first day of this new routine, Deb sticks her knuckle in the egg pile and gets pissy about it, flat out refuses it, so I vulture her leftovers, since I'm hungry but also dying for a non-jerky-like texture to work my jaws.

Deb realizes pretty quick that being a priss about perfectly fine food was going to get her nothing but a growling stomach, so she starts to welcome the cold eggs and toast with pleasure, showing Andrew her gratitude with a face-splitting smile and head-nodding and earnest moans.

Mostly Andrew and I measure survival foods in eensy-weensy portions, hardtack and jerky and all that. Before life was this eternal campout, before we hid from people and flipped our shit at even just a twig-snap underfoot, Andrew stocked up good, made sure what we had was portable and indestructible and could get us around well enough. My big part in this was stealing a dehydrator from a store in the shopping center, a home goods store I guess you'd call it. They sold crockpots and spatulas, too, ceramic creamers, oven mitts, and other bougie stuff. It was the dead end of winter and I had Andrew's black puffer coat, which goes way down to the knees, and besides I was five months along and that plus a dehydrator stuffed under your shirt are easy to overlook, as it happens. We filled the thing with muscly strips of deer and rabbit and other stuff that Andrew killed and I skinned. We let the vent whir, and we watched as some force slowly sucked on the meat until it went brown and twisty. We planned, planned, and planned, just the two of us.

I'm not pregnant anymore, so I can take some hardship. Deb gets special treatment because she is the youngest, Andrew explains. But I believe it is also because she has beautiful hair. Gorgeous, like just really stunning. These crazy springing curls that don't get matted and greasy like mine, but fall long down her back, so bleached white by the sun you could mistake her for albino if she didn't tan so good. Skin burnt sauce red, peeling off in pretty strips then turning so thoroughly golden that her white teeth and eyeballs and hair stand out more. She shines even now in the morning half light as she nibbles daintily on a point of bread. Andrew likes her so much because she is undeniable. I am ruddy, broad. I grow fur.

He used to watch her from across the street. Once he took me, too, to see her for myself. We parked around the corner behind a hedgerow, just out of sight, as she paraded around her front lawn. She had one of those kinds of batons, you know, with a sparkly blue wand and a length of ribbon coming out the top of it? She was a limber little gymnast, did cartwheels and tumbles down the sloping garden, stretching her body into a lanky *X* shape. Andrew leaned out the truck's driver side window and stuck out his first finger, the one I suck on like a cigarette candy, and he pointed at Deb on the lawn and, very taken with her, he said, "Well! Perfect for the Beautees."

When Andrew is feeling really great he talks about our group, a singing group called Andy Durrell (accent on the *–rell*) and the Bellevonia Beautees. Durrell was his mother's maiden name, and naturally Deb and I are the eponymous Beautees. Deb does her dancing and flopping around, and I have a beautiful singing voice. (This is not just a humble opinion of mine; people have actually said this to me. In the eleventh grade I got my own choral solo, a song called "Somewhere That's Green.") I want to make us swishy, lovely Lycra things to wear that really show off our figures, paint our lips and nails neon orange, wear white platform shoes. I wonder if it would be wise for me to get a blond wig, or if a wig would be made to look wiggier in comparison to the startling authenticity that is Deb's hair.

She will still shake and gambol around when I request of her some grandstanding, but there's no life in it anymore, even when I pinch behind her knee. Though of course she'll do anything Andrew asks, because she's learned that Andrew can be awful when he doesn't get things he asks, and he even bites. Which is funny, because weren't his first words to Deb, "Don't worry, I don't bite"?

His first to me were, "I never do this . . ." while he plucked a wayward bit of leaf from behind my ear like a magic coin. I promptly became a puddle of mush on the park bench. I still go warm and puddly down to my oats to think of it. Mom said the Beatles said that love's a long and winding road.

"TODAY WE NEED to pick up again," Andrew says as he crouches next to Deb's platter, nickels and quarters from Cassidy's tinkling out of his pocket, beef strip wadded in his cheek.

I say, "All right."

I do not say, "Oh fuck me Jesus." These pickups are always a bitch. They happen when Andrew is being a careless jackass, leaving a trace, maybe a Marlboro butt covered in curlicues of DNA, or stumbling across a hiker on his way down the mountain. Deb's picture is still all around town. Stapled to posts and hanging on a corkboard in the post office.

A couple days ago when he hoofed it back up to the tent he had one crumpled up his shirtsleeve. He flattened it over a rock: a shuddery black-and-white scan, a school picture, her hands lain primly on her skirt, her spectacular hair bound by a scrunchie, and eyes like cereal bowls, rimmed with black copy machine ink and thus made extra haunting. He showed it to her. "See, people are still looking for you, Debbie."

She didn't cry like he wanted. She zipped her lip.

But I said, "Hey, I'm going to pee," and I went far, far off. I folded myself into the hole of an oak and thought of Mom pulling a bristle brush through my hair, snarls of it in a black spider pile, sink filling with it. "Goddamn," she'd say through the pins in her teeth, "Monster baby, you are too too." Her spoonish hands wrangling a scrunchie and tying my bangs back like theater curtains, humming, "There we are. Ta-da! Prettiest things in Bellevonia."

Hunched in the tree, head full of her, I winced out a measly tear. But that was it. I was all out.

MOM WOULD SAY there's no time like the present, and there's no point in bitching about the picking up, so I might as well get to getting to. I pack up all our shit and push it back into our backpacks, squishing in trousers and hankies and sheets and the book about treating your woman kind until all the air's been squeezed out and every cranny's been used with utmost efficiency.

We go for miles. Too many more of his fuckups and these pickups and we'll have to eschew the mountain, the forest, flee Bellevonia for good. Andrew squints into the horizon and struts along with his walking stick, a crooked tree branch worn smooth, while I lug our things on my back. Andrew has the generator in one hand and, in the other, tin cups and water bottles latched on carabiners that clink together to a metallic beat. When for some mystical reason he feels the new spot is the new spot, I set down my heavy load. But! I still have the enviable task of resetting up the tent. Having done this a handful of times I've nearly gotten the hang of it, nailing stakes into earth scorched by summer, rude and crumbly, maneuvering plastic poles just right while Deb snorts into her hand to hide her laughter, help that she is, while I figure shit out, finagling ape-like.

"We're running out of food," I tell Andrew when I eyeball the rations. "We'll have to go into town. Maybe I should go if I'm less recognizable? Innocent damsel and all that? Bat my eyes?"

I bat my eyes for him as an example.

"No," he says.

"We got your coat in the sack. I'll slip in and shove some ramen up there, none the wiser."

"Sure, and it won't be at all suspicious, you wearing a big fuck-off coat in August, huh? Think I'm a lunk? Not letting you out so easy, baby."

Is it August already?

I'M PICKING JERKY crumbs from the slats in the dehydrator trays when Deb taps me on the shoulder and shoves a pillowcase in my face—the Beautee getup to make do before we get our hands on a decent ream of Lycra. It's show time. We wiggle out of our clothes and hike up the pillowcases, slit through the top, under our pits. Deb shows her back to me and gathers her curls over her shoulder as I knot the top of the case behind her back.

"Too tight!" she squeaks.

"Too bad," I say. He likes it tight.

"While the sun's shining, babies!" Andrew calls from the tent. He slaps a spatula against a metal pail and kicks out a four-four beat. "And a one, and a two," and "Oh, the shark, babe! Has such teeth, dear! And it shows them! Pearly white!"

We go about it: arm out, arm out, shake the rump. Leg out, leg out, thrust for three. Head jerk slide, head jerk kick, jumping jack and box step. Deb's feet are dragging as we shuffle up the dust. I whisper the time signature, but she doesn't seem to hear me.

"Just a jackknife!" (We do the *ooohs*.) "Has old MacHeath, babe." (*Ah-ooh*.)

"And he keeps it!" (*La-daa*) "Out of sight!"

Deb is huffy and puffy and keeps withering flat, so I pinch her. She quiets then, only mouths along as I get us bright and go-going. I get loud and loud and loud, I ripple through the crab grass. I shake the cliff. Let them hear me, let everybody hear.

Andrew cranes his ear against Deb's mouth as her lips flap away in soundless O shapes. He looks at me. I shrug and try to sing on, but he clenches his hand over my mouth and urges Deb, "Sing." I hold his hand against my face and keep shimmying my limbs as best I can. Deb stumbles in my shadow. He bares his teeth at her. Under his hand, I bare mine too. She goes, "Ooh, ooh." He points to the sun, and she shrieks the *oohs* piercing shrill, like the green warblers that skitter around in the treetops, praying to mate. Finally, finally, he beams with satisfaction and he gives her the look, that good look that filled my belly up, that look he used to save for me. The eyes that say, "God." The mouth that curls, "Rest." He ushers Deb into the tent and I pick a squat to cop way farther off, as far as I can get so as to not hear them but also still see the sunset. This sun is small and bloody but it sets fire to the skinny clouds, the whole sky, as it dips behind a stretch of spiky trees that eat it right up.

THE NEXT MORNING I expect to find him gone, as he's usually headed off to the diner by wake-up time, but then I remember that we are not where we once were, and that it's entirely possible the days of Cassidy's are behind us. I look over and see that Andrew is still dead asleep in his sleeping bag, a chunk of Deb's hair splayed snoozily over his shoulder. She's snoring to wake the devil, as usual. I turn to face the other side and slip my hands in prayer position under my ear, listening to warblers' chirps as I settle back to sleep. I'm not one to sniff at a lazy morning.

When I wake again it's to the smell of baked beans. I think, Does my nose deceive me? I think, Oh Heavenly Father.

Andrew is a few feet from the tent, a small fire blazing. And yes, he is heating a tin of beans, lid stabbed open, over its flame.

I cry, "Who died and made me bean queen?"

He says, "It's a good day, baby."

Deb has already tucked into a can of her very own, and gravy dribbles out the corners of her mouth onto her knee, which she scrapes with her finger and licks clean.

"What d'you say we *really* hunker down in the lap of luxury today, baby?"

"Come again?" I look behind both sides of me in a mock *who, me?* sort of gesture, but also I am genuinely befuddled.

"Let's get a room at the motel. I scoped it out earlier. Just under two miles south and a little west."

"The motel?"

"Pillows, babe."

"And a TV!" Deb squeals.

"And a TV, and a toilet with a seat and flusher."

"A porcelain throne for the queen of the beans."

"If you say so."

"How'd you find time to treat your woman so good? Women."

"I've got ways, baby, wicked and wonderful."

"That you do."

The first taste of real hot *hydrated* food in, what, weeks? I lower to my knees and let myself fall back on my butt, the wolf invited to the feast.

•

SOMETHING I SAID got through to him after all. I *am* less recognizable than him. For that reason he makes me put the room down, for one, under a fake name, so he and Deb can sneak through a side door down a ways while I distract the guy up front with some grab-bag story about my ex-husband finally signing those gosh-darn divorce papers and hell if I'm not taking to the road, destination anywhere, destination I don't care.

This guy has a creamy bread face and he keeps picking at a thing of whiteheads on his chin, saying, "You gotta be too young to be *divorced*," but he seems to enjoy the show anyway.

After a couple of minutes of that garbage I take the key from him and waggle my fingers, TTFN, thanks a billion!

I scurry down the hall to our room where Andrew and Deb are crouched in wait, shushing each other schoolgirlishly. Quietly, mouse quiet, I unlock the door, creak it open ever so slowly, and let them scamper in as I shut it behind us, just whisper it ever so gently into the jamb.

"Okay now, shh shh shh!" I scold them. Deb is going hog wild, jumping like nuts on the mattress, reaching her hands to the ceiling and lifting her face to the light like a plant. Even Andrew acts playful, grabbing her round the waist and twirling her from corner to corner and back again.

I quickly draw the curtains and insist that they shut up. I can't believe I'm the one playing zookeeper.

AS WE SETTLE into our temporary surroundings, sweetly remembered civilities float to the surface. Andrew switches on the TV, which briefly fizzes then fades into a program about how to make a yogurt parfait festive. He flips around, offering glimpses of shows about chimps, and one with an antique lamp the camera circles like a sexy dripping jewel, another with a woman in sepia overwhelmed by Tupperware. Deb curls against the yellow pillow with her chin hooked on her knees, potato bug in repose.

Over the course of the afternoon Andrew reveals more goodies. Bananas, green with tough peels but sweet and good, and some crunchy pieces of baguette, like where are we, France?

I call dibs on the bathroom, check myself out in the mirror. Hair knotted into ropes, teeth gapped, cheeks sunk, yes, scabbed, yes, but not nearly so bad as I thought. I take myself a long, hot shower. The grout in the tile is pink and black with various molds but I don't mind a tit. The water steams around me in a dream, fogging up the glass, on which I draw a fat heart with my finger. Comb my nails through my hair and rake my scalp, prickle and wriggle with pleasure at the feeling. Breathe in heat, hard, wet, warm, slick, clean, scrubbed, enveloped, and unraveled, pulled out like a loose red thread.

It almost pains me to turn off the faucet, but Deb knocks on the door and begs to do a number two. I sigh as I pick up a towel, rough and strangely stained but still a godsend, and tousle it through my hair, wrap it all up on top of my head like a shampoo commercial.

I open the door and the cold air goose-pimples my uncovered places. Steam billows out in big puffs.

Jeez, says Deb, and shuts the door behind her. She turns on the water in the sink, I assume so we won't hear the business of her shitting.

I collapse on the bed beside Andrew. "Really," I turn to him, "how'd you manage—?"

He gives me the most winning smile that pins up the corners of his mouth and cuts a dashing dimple in his cheek, a dimple I'd die to swim in, eyes like *U*'s upside down. He reaches out his palm, dry and strong and cool, and cups my cheek. I fall into it and rest like I'm rooted there.

The weather pops on, the week's forecast, Monday, Tuesday, Wednesday, all ninety or higher, so signified with smiley cartoon suns. So that's August 8, 9, etc., I deduce. Mom's birthday would've been Friday. Then the news, an anchor duo, and an announcement: "No updates on the disappearance of nine-year-old Deborah Hershey—"

I yank the towel from atop my head. Frenzy of footage of her parents, her mom a trembling Jell-O, her daddy on the rack, tears by the bucketful, phone number flashing across the bottom of the screen, cut to an enormous slab of a man sweating in his uniform, shaking his jowls into a microphone. I grab for the remote to turn it off, but Andrew snatches it back from me.

"Deb!" he yelps excitedly. "Deb, come out here, you gotta see this! Deb!"

He leaps up and dashes to the bathroom, rips open the door.

Deb screams and yells, "Hey!"

He pulls her to her feet and drags her out. She's naked from the waist down and covers herself modestly as if we haven't seen it already. She trips over her shorts, tangled around her ankles as Andrew circles her whole neck with his one hand and sits her in front of the TV screen.

"Would you look at that."

The same footage over and over again, in a frantic loop, of the police chief and Deb's parents, agape in their sorrow.

Deb contemplates the imagery. She steps out of her shorts and dirty panties and shuffles slowly to the screen, resting her fingers on top of the box and gazing intently, so close-up that the images are just blocks of color, red sweater and beige house, green lawn, black shirt, red and beige, green, black, and back again.

"See that, honey?" says Andrew, placing her into his lap at the foot of the bed. "They're looking for you. They're missing you something so fierce. Isn't that something? Isn't that something wonderful to see? Isn't it?"

All one had to do was squint, and shake one's head around and get a little something in one's eye, and it could look like it could be a bit like maybe those two at the foot of the bed, watching a show, could be a new family, and me too, the stern but loving head of it, a mom that combs her fingers through their hair in their sleep, shedding light and beauty, imparting incredible lessons as the fire spits on another magical evening. I try to see it, to see forever. The backs of my eyes are hot and ache with the trying.

Andrew regards me. I nod back *yes. Andrew, yes, it is wonderful.*

DEB IS SNORING into the crusty quilts she piled around her in a polyester mound, purring and so still.

"Time to pick up again tomorrow," Andrew whispers, and flaps the map, explaining it to me. "We'll have to continue north, out of Bellevonia totally, likely . . ." He points to a tree-colored clump about an inch long in a county I do not know. "Plenty of places to not be found there, yeah? After all, search for Deb still being on, leaving Bellevonia'd probably be for the best."

"No more Beautees?"

"Nah nah, drop the Bellevonia, keep the Beautees, till we're someplace no one's ever known us. *Then*"—he makes his hand an exploding star. "For now we got to practice, practice, practice. No good rusting."

That night I have one dream, a small one, about drinking a bowl of milk and getting a nosebleed and bleeding out my nose into the bowl. Otherwise I don't sleep a wink. Come morning my teeth are sore with heavy thinking.

I get up before them again, dig the bags out of the closet, and get to getting to. I fish around in Andrew's jean pockets and pick out a handful of quarters, stack them up in a pretty column on the tile floor, lay my clothes out on the brown grout. Looks like my body's melted and left them behind, or like I've been raptured up by the Big Man, or summoned somewhere I won't be needing them.

Step into the shower stall naked as the day I was born, but don't turn it on. Don't want to wake them. Shake my hair out and let it tickle my shoulders, so fresh and nice smelling, not matted or greasy, and I rake my fingers through it, smiling into the showerhead as if I intend to offer it my swan song. I picture forceful beads falling to my feet, torrential deafenings in my ear. Must get to getting to.

I haul our shit out to the parking lot, alone. The quarters sweat in my palm, and the phone booth smells like copper, and two quarters clink brightly in the slot, and I think of the numbers. I see them bright red and wriggling in my fingers. The fingers hook into the corresponding holes, one long drag and two quick clicks and the woman at the other end asks what is my emergency and whittles my heart down to a splinter. The sun is just a sliver. The clouds have fish-gray bellies, considering rain.

Lauren Friedlander is a graphic designer and writer from Kansas living in New York City. Find her on social media @la_friedlander.

EDITOR'S NOTE

As many a cowboy ballad can tell you, the halo glow of new love never lasts. Sometimes it simmers down with age; sometimes it flames into a new shape; and sometimes it just flickers out. It's one of those lessons most of us learn sooner or later.

Even so, every time I read "The Crazies" by Maud Streep, I can't help but be charmed by the halo glow of its early pages. The narrator, a recent college grad, heads to Montana, takes a job at a Wild West tourist attraction, and falls in love with a "cowboy" named Jake. Their marriage is a happy whirlwind of sex, cheap beer, optimism, and simple, carefree living.

But halfway through the story, the couple's happiness turns to anguish. Something terrible happens on an elk hunting trip in the Crazy Mountains, and the narrator and Jake may or may not be responsible. How each of them deals with this possibility will determine whether their love endures, or whether it flickers out.

"The Crazies" is wise about life and relationships in a manner one would expect from a veteran storyteller, not a debut author. Ditto for the prose, which sings with authority. Perhaps most striking of all, though, is Maud Streep's distinctive sensibility as a writer: one gets the sense that no one could have written this story the way she did.

Will Allison, contributing editor
One Story

THE CRAZIES

Maud Streep

I MET JAKE working at a ghost town in western Montana the summer I turned twenty-two. I had just graduated from Yale and was "doing something different." Jake played a cowboy, and my best friend Liza and I played whores. We leaned over wooden balconies to holler at the tourists, our white cotton chemises pulled low over corset-hoisted boobs. Every day at noon and four, Jake broke up a gunfight in the street while Liza and I fanned our jaded faces. We bunked in a long-stay motel at the edge of town and spent our nights drinking in our rooms, on the roof, in the parking lot out back. I'd sit by Jake and feel the space between us go live.

One night we hit an emergency: Liza ran out of cigarettes. Jake had bummed too many the night before. I told him I would come along for the ride. We were still in our work clothes, so after I'd backed him up against the door of his truck, and after he'd helped me into its bed, it took some concentration to lose the chaps and stays. And then, naked behind the gas station in the light-stained August twilight, free from all that, I thought: I could wear this sweat forever.

Liza headed for San Francisco when summer ended, but I loved Montana with the passion of a convert. Jake and I moved to Bozeman, got married, and bought a little clapboard house. My grandmother's bequest took care of the down payment. He started the customer service position he'd lined up at Simms, the big fishing gear company in town, and I got hired as a receptionist at a doctor's office. It turned out I was okay having a job that was just a job. His parents were happy to have us so close to them, and I was happy to be far from mine.

Here's how we used to be: we drove all the way to Missoula just to go dancing. We went skinny-dipping in cold green swimming holes, and we drank cheap beer. We ate our trout fried with the salt and pepper we kept in little baggies tucked in our fly boxes. I tuned out all day at work, and when I got home, Jake poured our drinks and read books out loud. Even now my mother enjoys telling me we got married too young, as if that hadn't been the idea all along.

BY THE TIME Jake took me hunting, we'd been married just over a year. Our first fall, he and his cousin Mike went as usual and split the elk they brought home. I learned to make elk burgers, elk steaks, elk chilies, elk stews. All winter, I'd throw on a sweater to root around in the mudroom's big meat freezer and feel a little thrill of competence. If by summer I was ready to eat anything but elk, I kept it to myself.

Our second fall, Jake sent Mike his regrets. We agreed to call in sick one Friday in early November. We drove past Big Timber and didn't stop for lunch. I'd packed sandwiches and pickles. Jake turned up a road he knew, and we bumped along past rich person ranches and real ranches. We listened to this tape we'd made with Loretta Lynn on one side and Gram Parsons on the other. I rolled down the window and smelled dung and cold air. Jake dropped a little sandwich meat on his jeans. The road got worse. Beside us I caught movement—a small bear. Jake slowed the truck, and I watched the animal's weight move up and down. It looked like it was running in slow motion, the way the flesh fell under all that fur, but the bear kept pace with the truck. It scared me, how fast it was. It didn't look clumsy or soft. It cut off to the right and disappeared into the tall dead grass.

"Go to sleep already, jeez," I said. I ate another pickle.

We turned a corner and saw the face of Crazy Peak. It looked like a mountain in a textbook—a blunted gray triangle trailing into a ridge on one side. It had snow in its gullet. Out the window, past Jake, the meadow sloped gold down to dark trees and a creek. "Let's move *here*," I said. "Build me a shack."

"You know, these used to be called the Crazy Woman Mountains," Jake said. "That's where the name comes from."

"The name's because they're not part of the Rockies."

"Nope. There was this pioneer lady. Her whole family was massacred. Every single one. She wandered around up here for years. People took care of her—mountain men, that kind of thing. They'd leave food. And the local tribes left her alone after that. She never talked, but folks around here say that even now you can hear her wailing at night."

"Keening," I said.

"Would you keen for me?" he said. "If I was brutally murdered?"

Jake had crooked teeth. His eyes were green, and he never fully lost his tan. That first summer, Liza and I had code-named him Dangerface.

"If you brutally stole someone else's land, you mean? Hard to say."

"You would," he said, sliding his hand up my thigh.

I swatted him and said, "Watch the road, bud." He slid his hand a little higher. We stopped off on the side of the road and he shimmied my jeans down in the front seat. I closed my eyes but kept seeing that bear, so I opened them and looked down to where Jake's head moved between my legs, out to the blank sky beyond him. My mind wouldn't empty. I pulled him up to me.

We hiked into the foothills. I didn't pay much attention to where we were. In a high pasture, we saw some straggling cattle. There was nothing human around us. Even though fall was on its way out, it hadn't really snowed yet. My pack hurt my shoulders.

Jake set up the winter tent. I liked it because it was orange. It made us look like an Arctic expedition. I started a fire and wrapped potatoes in tinfoil to stick down in the coals.

Jake took out my rifle and made me show him that I remembered how to use it. We'd shot cans and bottles in the summer. I loved the rifle's heft in my arms, its clockwork insides, the way the bullet's force echoed back into my shoulder. I didn't tell my mother how much I liked the gun or how much it frightened me. I just told her I was a good shot.

Now I loaded it and checked the safety and aimed it and unloaded it. When Jake was satisfied, he opened the whiskey. "We can go in the early morning or the late afternoon," he said, passing the bottle. "Your call. I've had luck in the valley just over the ridge."

"How're we going to get the meat out of here? Aren't they huge?" I had never seen an up-close elk that wasn't freezer ready or a head on a wall.

"It'll take a couple trips." He picked up his knife and waggled it at me. "Don't worry, I'll handle the gross part. But yeah, they're huge. And smart. We'll need to go slow and be really, really quiet. You keep one in the chamber—any little sound is gonna spook them."

"Let's go in the afternoon," I said. "Let's sleep late and make out."

"You don't have to come if you don't want," he said. "You can hang out in camp. Look at the trees."

"Sing to the birds. Talk to the foxes."

"No guns necessary." He wrapped his arms around me.

I shook him off. "We're teaching me to hunt."

WE WENT IN the afternoon. I walked the way Jake showed me, slow and steady, with bent knees. The gun was heavy, though, and I knew I wasn't as quiet as I should be. I tried to look around and see the signs that Jake was reading, but all I could think about was the rifle across my chest. I had this fear that I hadn't really put the safety on, like when I don't believe I locked the front door, even though I remember locking it, and then when I go back to check it, I have to unlock it and lock it all over again. Now I knew that somehow the gun would go off and I would accidentally murder my husband and no matter what I pressed into the wound the blood would keep coming and Jake would fade out and his eyes would go still and I would be alone in the woods with bears and the ghost of a mourning woman. That's where my head was; I wasn't thinking about elk. I kept my eyes on Jake's orange back or on the ground in front of my feet.

We came over the ridge and the air turned cloying. Jake raised a hand to slow me. He nodded. I wasn't looking at the ground anymore. We slowed even further. Through the trees, I was pretty sure

I could see something moving. The smell closed in again, musky and physical. My body remembered we were here to kill.

The blood in my ears drummed me forward. My limbs went light; each step landed without sound.

When I try to pin down this feeling now, three things come to mind. I remember the first time Jake took me fishing, the recognition in my arm as I hit a perfect cast. I remember the purpose with which I held my grandmother's paper-thin Dresden teacup above my head, my delight in its fall. I remember kicking a boy in the face.

I felt clear. I was made for this.

But then Jake waved me forward, the smallest tug of a finger on air, a trigger pull. I panicked: I didn't want to know more. I wanted out of the woods, back in the truck, ten minutes, two days earlier, anything to scrub the blood before it hit my hands. I looked for a root at the base of the nearest pine and tripped myself as hard as I could.

I said, "Ow, ow, ow."

I wasn't quiet.

Any nearby animal would be gone now. I felt a funny mix of relief and shame. Jake jogged back to me and crouched to inspect. My knee bled through my pants, so I rolled up the leg. The scrape was shallow but a gusher. He tilted his flask, and whiskey hit the open skin.

"Jesus, no more falling with loaded guns, huh?" he said. He looked rattled, which scared me. I could have shot open his skull. I could have shot off my foot. This was how I'd call the ghost—not by accident but because of a dumb mistake. I hadn't even checked the safety.

"I'm sorry I ruined everything," I said. "I'm an idiot. I'm sorry."

He sat down on the dirt next to me. He kissed my hand and rubbed my fingers to warm them up.

"I didn't really think we'd get lucky today. The wind's shifting around a lot. I'm sure they smelled us coming."

We picked our way down to the valley anyway. The ground was pocked with the elks' wide beds. The scent was inescapable, with a new sourness layered in. I looked at the wallows and tried to fill in the bodies that had lain there.

We spent another night in camp. When dawn broke, I made a fire and some coffee, and Jake broke down the tent. The wind was cold and fierce, and we didn't see a reason to linger. In the car, I tried to gauge the disappointment in Jake's face until I got bored of that and looked out the window instead. I had wanted to be the kind of wife who'd bring down an elk one day and cook it the next, in lingerie and a flannel shirt. I thought, This is a test and you are getting through it. I am myself and that self will be okay.

THAT NIGHT AT the bar, I made us sit across from the elk mount: I faced my failure head-on.

"Stop apologizing. It's never a sure thing. And I can always try again next weekend with Mike," Jake said. "You look cute with a gun, though."

"Ew." I kicked him a little under the table. He grabbed my leg. He seemed so unbothered—I wondered if the trip had been a trial run all along.

Nearby, someone said, "Pretty late for a fire."

We looked up. The television behind the bar filled with flames and milky night sky. The silhouette of a house shifted and danced. White lettering read *Fire in the Crazies*. I stood up.

"Where are you going?" Jake said.

The television said "driving winds" and "fighting for control." It showed men in fire hats, black smudges against the pale red. It said "foothills near Big Timber."

"I guess we got lucky after all," Jake said. "Could have been a gnarly exit."

"Wind conditions," the television said again. It showed an old man looking dazed. The image switched to a newscaster in a studio and then back to a high school basketball game.

I made Jake take me home. In the car, I scanned the radio for more news.

"Fires happen out here," he said. "Let it go."

That morning, we'd left behind an ember that kindled a fire that burned sixteen thousand acres, two homes, thirteen outbuildings, and a small historical society. We killed seventy-two cows and countless small animals. I'll always believe this.

IT TOOK TWO days to get the fire under control. I stayed up late, checking the *Billings Gazette* website for their slow updates and watching the estimates change: the acreage shrank while the building count climbed. When they announced the historical society on Monday morning, I took another sick day. The news of the cattle came later that afternoon. The paper ran some lines from a woman who said, "I wish it had taken the house."

When Jake came home that night, I was sitting with my knees pulled up at the kitchen table. A topographical map draped over some plates. The radio was on. I felt drawn and sallow in the glow of the computer. I was wearing his robe. "Is everything okay?" he said.

I closed my laptop. "It's snowing at least. They think that's going to help."

"Did you go to work today?" He walked over slow and quiet, like we were back out hunting.

"We have to tell the police or someone."

"Tell them what?" He set his bag down and drew out the chair across from me.

I should have fixed my hair. It occurred to me I was unconvincing with it greasy and pulled up on top of my head like that. I could see in his face what I looked like.

"They're trying to figure out what started the fire," I said.

"You think *we* did."

"Yes, Jake, we obviously started it."

I'd spent all day reconstructing that morning coffee at the camp. I hadn't made a big fire, just one to get some warmth in us before we began the long way out. I could see it, the little square cabin I'd built from the night's leftover kindling and a few small logs. I was proud of how fast I got it going, as if that could make up for my ineptitude the day before. I remembered dumping the coffee grounds over the hissing coals. The rest was like whether I'd locked the front door: the more I went over it, the more artificial the whole thing became. Had I mixed it with dirt, stirred it till it was good and cold and dead? I could picture myself doing it, but the picture looked false.

Jake put both his hands on the table and stretched out his fingers and closed them up again. He took a breath as if he were dealing with a little kid.

"That seems like a big leap," he said. "Did they say it was human-caused?"

"It's still under investigation. But come on, did you notice any lightning out there? It's November."

"I think we should let them investigate. We don't want to confuse things."

"It seems like relevant information that we were in the area the day the fire started, and you know, had a *fire* going."

"Everybody's hunting right now. I seriously doubt we were the only people up there," Jake said. "Did they get more specific about where it started?"

Outside the window, snow blew by. I wondered if it melted down to water when it neared the flames or went straight to steam.

I said, "I don't understand why we shouldn't at least tell them we were in the area."

Jake chewed the skin by his thumbnail. "What's the damage looking like?"

I tried to keep my voice even as I told him about the historical society. I like old things. I like people trying to preserve what's past. We'd driven by it on our way back, and I'd wanted to stop. It was a beat-up, whitewashed, one-room schoolhouse, worn and Western in exactly the way that used to catch me up. The real-life evidence of our costume drama. The papers said some photographs had been on loan to the neighboring library, so at least they were saved.

Jake came around the table. He held my head against his belly and stroked my hair. I let him take me upstairs.

I WOKE IN the night, surprised I had fallen asleep at all. The maple out back banged against the house, and the moon was white across our bed. The wind had carried the snow to someplace else. Jake pushed himself up next to me. We sat side by side, cross-legged under our bright comforter.

"I can't remember putting out the fire," I said.

"You did. I saw you." He rubbed his face. "Listen, it's like this out here. Things burn."

When we bought the house, Jake told me settlers had planted the maples to remind their East Coast wives of home. I suspected the men holding the money planted the trees for their own benefit, and I didn't see why they were the settlers while their wives were just wives, but I hadn't asked questions. I liked his story, the snug nesting boxes he built for us.

"Show me exactly where we were on the map." I swung my legs out of bed, but Jake put a hand to my back.

"You know they fine like a million dollars for this kind of thing? Is your inheritance gonna cover that too?"

"Seventy-two cows," I said.

"Jesus, what an overdeveloped sense of guilt. I bet you've eaten that many in your lifetime anyway." His mouth stayed tight but his eyes lit for a moment, pleased at his own humor.

"There's something wrong with you," I said. "You're morally deficient."

Jake chewed at his thumb. The maple drew wild, shifting lines across our legs. From the beginning, I'd believed that when we peeled back the cowboy and the whore, the waders and Wranglers and whiskey, at the center we'd be there, together, outlines bold and clear.

Here we were.

"Let's go away," he said. "Let's get drunk in some motel room out in the middle of nowhere."

I went downstairs to look at the map alone.

IN THE MORNING, I showered and dried my hair, put on a nice sweater, and drove to work at the doctor's office. I parked in the lot but left the engine running. When I called Debbie, the other receptionist, to say this fever was still going and would she be willing to cover for me again, she said, "Oh, honey. You bet."

I drove with the heat on and the windows cracked, winter hitting my face. A few miles out of Big Timber, I smelled it. Since moving out west, I'd gotten used to the summer fire season, the heavy air and blurred sun, the headaches and the lethargy. Hanging in the cold sky, this smoke smelled different. It smelled cleaner, more benevolent, like campfire. I followed the haze up the smaller highway that Jake had taken. It got thicker, and the smell did too. Near Melville, I stopped the car and pushed open the door to watch ash fall around me, like snow.

No one was at the spot where the historical society used to be. Its charred stubs rested on charred ground, protected by yellow tape and a fine white dusting. I'd expected crowds and urgency, something I could help with, maybe. A ranger to tell me they'd found the culprit and guess what, it wasn't me. I picked at the loose threads of my coat cuffs. My throat got small. I wondered how long it would be before the tall grass moved back in, remembered gold stalks closing behind that bear. I took a little burnt-up stick and put it in my pocket.

THE DIVORCE WAS about as cut-and-dried as those things get. He'd wanted to drive to Reno, pull some Merle Haggard if-we're-not-back-in-love-by-Monday stunt, but I insisted we file in Bozeman: I was done with country romance. He kept the house, and I kept what was left of my inheritance. I flew to San Francisco, stayed with Liza until I got my feet on the ground.

•

THIS WAS ALL years ago. My second husband and I live down in L.A. now. Is that what I ought to call him? Current husband? Forever husband? We have good friends, a 1920s cottage, a garden filled with drought-resistant plants. He's a screenwriter, and I'm a specialist at an auction house. I got the long-intended art history degree, fulfilled the familial destiny. I never became a vegetarian. When the forever husband asks me for a Montana story, I know what he's looking for. He wants horses and high plains. He wants me in Dale Evans drag, suede skirt swinging.

I tell him about a DMV where everyone is pleasant and the entire errand, whatever the errand may be, takes only half an hour.

That winter—after the fire, before the divorce—I retreated indoors. I spent hours googling wildfires, negligence, fines, then made sure to clear the search history so Jake wouldn't see. I could feel him tugging and pushing at my edges, trying so hard to fit us back into the people we thought we were. By the time the rivers melted, he settled on his official response—talking points about the lodgepole pine and fire-dependent ecosystems—and I stopped bringing up the fire.

Once, I drove to the police station and sat outside in my car. I told myself I'd follow the first person I saw go in, then the third, then the fifth. I watched people move in and out until my fingers went bloodless and yellow on the wheel. When I started the engine, I believed it was for Jake.

Once, I put an anonymous tip in an envelope and stood in our kitchen with the glue's dry sweetness on my tongue. Out in the yard, matted grass showed through the thaw. Bear, ground squirrels, artifacts, cattle. I lit the envelope in our sink. Fire shot up so fast I had to jump back, and my fingertips felt hot and solid where I'd held on too close. I smelled the match, but no smoke. The flames ate the paper down to a curled ghost.

Maud Streep is from Nyack, New York, and lives in Brooklyn. A 2017 NYC Emerging Writers Fellow at the Center for Fiction, she has received scholarships and fellowships from the Bread Loaf Writers' Conference, Lighthouse Works, VCCA, Djerassi, and Yaddo. She holds an MFA from the University of Montana.

ABOUT THE JUDGES

JODI ANGEL is the author of two story collections, *The History of Vegas* and *You Only Get Letters from Jail*, which was named a Best Book of 2013 by *Esquire*. Her work has appeared in *Esquire*, *Tin House*, *One Story*, *Zoetrope: All-Story*, Electric Literature's *Recommended Reading*, and *Byliner*, among other publications and anthologies. Her short story "Snuff" was selected for inclusion in *The Best American Mystery Stories 2014*. She lives in northern California with a pack of dogs.

LESLEY NNEKA ARIMAH is a Nigerian writer born in the UK and currently living in Minneapolis. She won The 2017 Kirkus Prize for Fiction, was a finalist for the John Leonard Prize, and was named a "5 under 35" honoree by the National Book Foundation for her debut story collection *What It Means When a Man Falls from the Sky*. Her stories have appeared in *The New Yorker*, *Harper's Magazine*, *Granta*, *Catapult*, and other publications, and she has received grants and awards from Commonwealth Writers, AWP, the Elizabeth George Foundation, the Jerome Foundation, and others.

ALEXANDRA KLEEMAN is a Staten Island–based writer of fiction and nonfiction, and the winner of the 2016 Bard Fiction Prize. Her fiction has been published in *The New Yorker*, *The Paris Review*, *Zoetrope: All-Story*, *Conjunctions*, and *Guernica*, among others. Nonfiction essays and reportage have appeared in *Harper's Magazine*, *Tin House*, *n+1*, and *The Guardian*. Her work has received scholarships and grants from Bread Loaf, the Virginia Center for the Creative Arts, Santa Fe Art Institute, and ArtFarm Nebraska. She is the author of the novel *You Too Can Have a Body Like Mine* and the story collection *Intimations*.

ABOUT THE PEN/ROBERT J. DAU SHORT STORY PRIZE FOR EMERGING WRITERS

The PEN/Robert J. Dau Short Story Prize for Emerging Writers recognizes twelve fiction writers for a debut short story published in a print or online literary magazine. The annual award was offered for the first time during PEN's 2017 awards cycle.

The twelve winning stories are selected by a committee of three judges. Each winning writer receives a $2,000 cash prize and is honored at the annual PEN Literary Awards Ceremony in New York City. Every year, Catapult will publish the winning stories in *PEN America Best Debut Short Stories*.

This award is generously supported by the family of the late Robert J. Dau, whose commitment to the literary arts has made him a fitting namesake for this career-launching prize. Mr. Dau was born and raised in Petoskey, a city in Northern Michigan in close proximity to Walloon Lake where Ernest Hemingway had spent his summers as a young boy and which serves as the backdrop for Hemingway's *The Torrents of Spring*. Petoskey is also known for being where Hemingway determined that he would commit to becoming a writer. This proximity to literary history ignited the Dau family's interest in promoting emerging voices in fiction and spotlighting the next great American fiction writer.

LIST OF PARTICIPATING PUBLICATIONS

PEN America and Catapult gratefully acknowledge the following publications, which published debut fiction in 2017 and submitted work for consideration to the PEN/Robert J. Dau Short Story Prize.

805 Lit + Art
African Voices
Alfred Hitchcock's Mystery Magazine
American Chordata
Apogee
Atlantis Short Story Contest
The Baltimore Review
Bellevue Literary Review
Black Warrior Review
Bomb
The Brooklyn Review
Carve Magazine
The Chattahoochee Review
The Cincinnati Review
Cleaver Magazine
The Collagist
Conjunctions
Cosmic Roots and Eldritch Shores
Cosmonauts Avenue
Crab Creek Review
Culture Trip

Ellery Queen's Mystery Magazine
Epiphany
Epoch
Evergreen Review
Exposition Review
Fields
Fifth Wednesday Journal
Fireside
Fiyah
The Forge
F(r)iction
Fugue
FWJ Plus
Glimmer Train
Gravel
The Greensboro Review
Harvard Review
Hunger Mountain
The Inquisitive Eater
Jelly Bucket
J Journal
Joyland
Juked
Kenyon Review
Lady Churchill's Rosebud Wristlet
The Literary Review
Longshot Island
The Malahat Review
The Massachusetts Review
The Masters Review

McSweeney's
Moonchild Magazine
The Moth
New England Review
New Limestone Review
Nimrod
Ninth Letter
NOON
North American Review
One Story
One Teen Story
Outlook Springs
Oxford American
The Paris Review
Philadelphia Stories
Ploughshares
A Public Space
Reckoning
Recommended Reading
Rigorous
The Rumpus
Slice
Somesuch Stories
Sonora Review
Straylight Magazine
Subtropics
The Sun
Tennessee Bar Journal
Tin House
The Tishman Review

Tupelo Quarterly
Washington Square Review
Western Humanities Review
Wigleaf
Witness

PERMISSIONS

"1983" by Elinam Agbo. First published in *The Baltimore Review*, Fall 2017. Copyright © 2017 by Elinam Agbo. Reprinted by permission of the author.

"Bellevonia Beautee" by Lauren Friedlander. First published in *The Rumpus*, April 12, 2017. Copyright © 2017 by Lauren Friedlander. Reprinted by permission of the author.

"New Years in La Calera" by Cristina Fríes. First published in *Epoch* Volume 66, Number 3, 2017. Copyright © 2017 by Cristina Fríes. Reprinted by permission of the author.

"Appetite" by Lin King. First published in *Slice* Issue 21, Fall 2017/Winter 2018. Copyright © 2017 by Lin King. Reprinted by permission of the author.

"Zombie Horror" by Drew McCutchen. First published in *The Baltimore Review*, Spring 2017. Copyright © 2017 by Drew McCutchen. Reprinted by permission of the author.

"Six Months" by Celeste Mohammed. First published in *New England Review* Volume 38, Number 1, 2017. Copyright © 2017 by Celeste Mohammed. Reprinted by permission of the author.

"Brent, Bandit King" by Grayson Morley. First published in *The Brooklyn Review*, Spring 2017. Copyright © 2017 by Grayson Morley. Reprinted by permission of the author.

"The Crazies" by Maud Streep. First published in *One Story* Issue 234, November 14, 2017. Copyright © 2017 by Maud Streep. Reprinted by permission of the author.

"Black Dog" by Alex Terrell. First published in *Black Warrior Review*, Fall/Winter 2017. Copyright © 2017 by Alex Terrell. Reprinted by permission of the author.

“Videoteca Fin del Mundo” by Ava Tomasula y Garcia. First published in *Black Warrior Review*, Spring/Summer 2017. Copyright © 2017 by Ava Tomasula y Garcia. Reprinted by permission of the author.

“Candidates” by Megan Tucker. First published in *Washington Square Review* Issue 40, Fall 2017. Copyright © 2017 by Megan Tucker. Reprinted by permission of the author.

“Stay Brave, My Hercules” by Ernie Wang. First published in *McSweeney’s* Issue 51, December 2017. Copyright © 2017 by Ernie Wang. Reprinted by permission of the author.

PEN America stands at the intersection of literature and human rights to protect open expression in the United States and worldwide. The organization champions the freedom to write, recognizing the power of the word to transform the world. Its mission is to unite writers and their allies to celebrate creative expression and defend the liberties that make it possible.

PEN.ORG